Bequia sweet, sweet

A tribute and guide to the island of Bequia in the St Vincent Grenadines

Pat Mitchell

On Bequia . . . is a blackbird, a new
species named the *Quiscalus Luminosus*,
which makes the air respond with its
joyous cry: 'Bequia sweet, sweet,
Bequia sweet!'

Frederic A Ober,
Camps in the Caribbees, 1880

**MACMILLAN
CARIBBEAN**

First published 1994

Published by THE MACMILLAN PRESS LTD
London and Basingstoke
*Associated companies and representatives in Accra,
Auckland, Delhi, Dublin, Gaborone, Hamburg, Harare,
Hong Kong, Kuala Lumpur, Lagos, Manzini, Melbourne,
Mexico City, Nairobi, New York, Singapore, Tokyo.*

ISBN 0-333-60952-2

Typeset by Florencetype Ltd, Kewstoke, Avon, UK
Printed in Hong Kong

A catalogue record for this book is available from the
British Library.

To my daughters, Sabrina, Gretel and Louise,
and to Son, who brought us here

Heading home from school, Paget Farm

ACKNOWLEDGEMENTS

I am grateful to the good people of Bequia and to the many others who helped with this book.

Richard Dey kindly allowed us to include the poem *Bequia Sweet* from his collection *Bequia Poems* (published by The Macmillan Press); Nathalie Ward permitted us to use a number of her fine whaling photographs.

Many people took the time to talk to me. Amelia Duncan, Athneal Ollivierre, Griffith Ollivierre, Jeff Gregg and friends, Daphne Grant, Kathleen Frederick, Olsen Peters, Wilfred Dederer, Anthony Blunden and Janni Jansen are among those who provided useful information.

Elaine Ollivierre wisely commented on the text; Curtis Ollivierre provided transportation.

Special thanks to the Rt Hon J F Mitchell, Ian and Cyrilene Gale, Lavinia Gunn and Michael Bourne for their early and continuing support for the project.

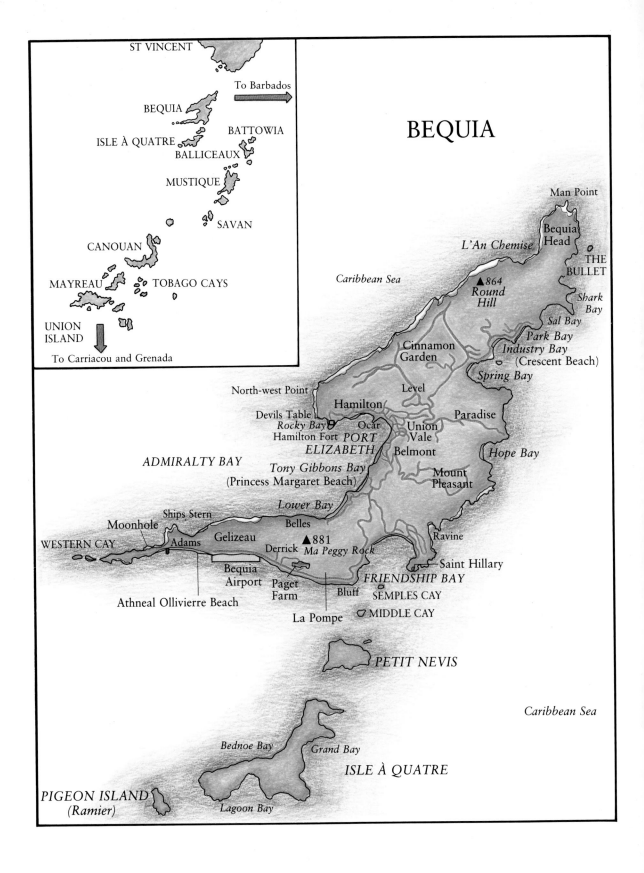

ST VINCENT

To Barbados

BEQUIA

ISLE À QUATRE

BATTOWIA

BALLICEAUX

MUSTIQUE

SAVAN

CANOUAN

MAYREAU   TOBAGO CAYS

UNION
ISLAND

To Carriacou and Grenada

BEQUIA

Man Point

Bequia
Head

L'An Chemise

THE
BULLET

*Shark
Bay*

Caribbean Sea

▲864
*Round
Hill*

Sal Bay

Park Bay
Industry Bay
(Crescent Beach)

Spring Bay

Cinnamon
Garden

Level

North-west Point

Hamilton

Paradise

Devils Table
Rocky Bay
Hamilton Fort
*PORT
ELIZABETH*

Ocar

Union
Vale

Belmont

Mount
Pleasant

Hope Bay

ADMIRALTY BAY

Tony Gibbons Bay
(Princess Margaret Beach)

Lower Bay

Belles

Ravine

Moonhole

Ships Stern

Gelizeau

▲881
Ma Peggy Rock

Saint Hillary

WESTERN CAY

Adams

Derrick

FRIENDSHIP BAY

Bequia
Airport

Paget
Farm

Bluff

SEMPLES CAY

Athneal Ollivierre Beach

La Pompe

MIDDLE CAY

PETIT NEVIS

Caribbean Sea

Bednoe Bay

Grand Bay

ISLE À QUATRE

*PIGEON ISLAND
(Ramier)*

Lagoon Bay

Contents

Foreword

Before 1969, when electricity came to Bequia, when we wanted to be sure of some ice for a drink we had to hustle an empty crocus bag to the 6.30 am ferry and beg one of the crew to bring us a hundred-pound block from town. We were resigned to its arrival in less than prime condition, probably a third sucked up by the solar-heated deck, and possibly a few chips gone into a whisky chaser for the boys. It was not unknown for a clever passenger to rest a strap of fish on it for ready refrigeration during the crossing.

Before 1970, when we were first blessed with telephones, if we needed something from the Mainland we sent a little note, or 'scrip', by a friendly ferryman who would drop it at the appropriate merchant. If the item did not arrive that afternoon on the one boat of the day we had no way of knowing whether the note had ever reached its destination, whether it had been delivered but the item was unavailable, whether the goods had been lost in transit or whether the system had broken down somewhere else along the way. It often took several 'scrips' and as many days to secure a single item from St Vincent.

In 1966, when I first came to Bequia, there were generally more cargo schooners than yachts in the bay. To keep in touch with an outside world, seemingly very distant, we cherished the BBC on our little short-wave transistor.

It is easy to feel nostalgic for that slow-moving Bequia of the old days, to wish life were a video one could rewind, stop, and replay, savouring it all again. Instead we lunge ahead now, perpetually it seems, in fast forward.

One of the purposes of this book is to record the blend of old and new that is Bequia today. Men and women, for example, patiently pound stone with a hammer turning rocks into mounds of gravel just a few yards from the modern new airport. Before the moon rises, a fisherman holds a flambeau, a burning kerosene-dipped rag in a bottle, before the bow of his

Mending a seine net near the airport

little boat to attract bait, which he scoops up with a dip net. Not far away Bequia-owned fishing trawlers twenty times his size are resting at anchor, their bait a scientifically prepared import from the United States.

This state of transition can be unsettling. Values are uncertain. New problems have arisen, while some of the old ones remain unsolved.

Yet Bequia is holding her own. A special charm brings visitors back year after year, and seduces many a newcomer almost instantly.

The blackbirds here say, 'Bequia sweet, sweet!' over and over and over – a sentiment with which many of us would agree. If occasionally the final note of the birdsong seems, by its rising intonation, to be posing a question, that too is in order. Nowhere on earth is a paradise, despite the calypso.

Photographs, by their nature, stop the clock at a particular moment in time. Most of those reproduced here were taken in the past two years. They witness a beauty, strength, grace and spirit that future generations of Bequians will have to work hard to retain, hopefully with the help of leaders who take the right development decisions, and with the continuing feisty devotion of Bequia lovers at home and around the world.

Pat Mitchell
Bequia, 1993

Walkway along the bayside at Belmont, Admiralty Bay

At the small dinghy dock, Port Elizabeth

Welcome to Bequia

The visitor's first impression of Bequia, whether from the deck of the ferry boat as it rounds the point into the wonderfully sheltering harbour of Admiralty Bay or from the window of the twin-engine plane as it veers down to landing past the fishing village of Paget Farm, is apt to be one, above all, of gentleness. Softly undulating hills, colourfully painted houses pressed on to protecting slopes, delicate curves of sand, vessels bobbing at anchor – these simple sights kindle, somehow, a sense of well-being. Not a few strangers have decided then and there that this is it – their own special place away from home.

Perhaps the important factor is size. A diverse island of only seven square miles, Bequia is too small for big industrial projects or super-highways, yet large enough to offer the basic needs – other people, shops and services, and space to 'get away from it all' on occasion. Bequia is on a scale to which human beings can relate, naturally, and with ease.

And size has, no doubt, determined the character of her people. Driven by the necessity of securing most commodities from abroad, Bequia men have looked to the sea for their living – as merchant seamen on world-travelling freighters, as captains and crews on cargo ships of the region or on yachts and cruise ships traversing the world, and as fishermen and lobster divers supplying local needs or exporting to other islands. Men of the sea have an independent way of looking at life, as do the women who hold the fort during their often long absences, tending the home, the land and the children, without the security of a man's daily presence to rely on.

Not only sailors but also many other Bequians over the years have looked abroad to find their fortune. Every Bequia family has close relatives in England, Canada or the United States. Many major cities there have Vincentian organisations; among those in New York is the Bequia United Progressive Organization. These emigrants do not forget their roots. They return when they can with all the latest news and styles, or they send parcels, cassettes and money orders to their loved ones on 'the Rock'.

As much as Bequians have always looked outwards, strangers have been fascinated by this little island. Initially the attraction was Bequia's magnificent harbour. The merchant and royal navies of the Dutch, the Spanish, the French and the English, who fought in the sixteenth, seventeenth and eighteenth centuries for control of the valuable Caribbean, sought shelter here. Cannon at Hamilton Fort on Admiralty Bay's north-west point bear the French fleur-de-lis. Old maps of the region show Bequia charted long before it was known that California was not an island. Early this century New England whaling ships made stops in Bequia to recruit the hardy local sailors as crew.

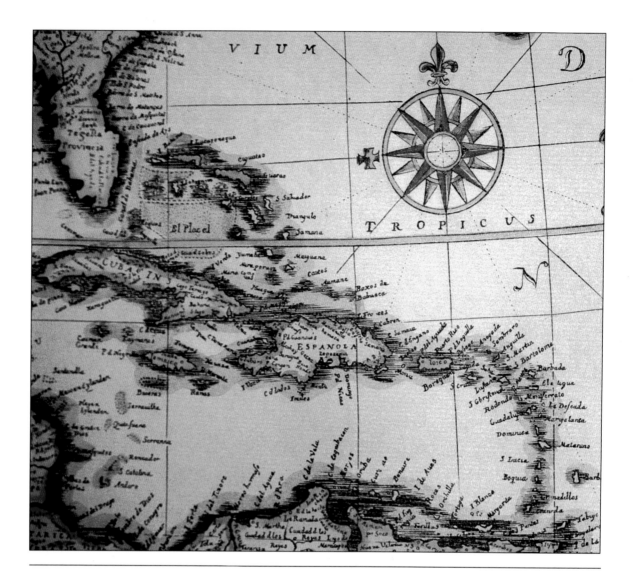

Part of a map produced in Amsterdam in 1631 clearly marks Bequia, although there is no sign of St Vincent

In modern times yachts and cruise ships from all over the world drop anchor in the harbour. The occasional British warship or French minesweeper may be seen showing the flag, taking respite from less amenable climes or simply relaxing in the pleasant bay.

The historic interest of seafarers in Bequia has recently been matched by the interest of tourists who come as much for the island as the sea. Now, if they like, they can arrive by air at the new airstrip opened in 1992.

A Bequia dinghy passes the tourist ship Mandalay

The Bequia Airport, a European assisted project, was built entirely on reclaimed land by Dutch contractors with German consultants

This continuing interchange over the years, this flow of people and ideas – the Bequia seamen and emigrants moving out (and returning), the yachtsmen and tourists visiting (and sometimes staying) – has resulted in a population more sophisticated than that of many larger islands. Bequia people are accustomed to strangers. They will look at you intently – anyone new in a small place is food for the eye – but this is the result of interest, not mistrust. In fact, the relationship between Bequians and visitors is the island's greatest asset, one that we must hope will continue allowing Bequia to remain what it is now to so many people – a very special place.

Claude Victorine, a native of France who has made her home in Bequia, paints on silk in her studio at Lower Bay (ABOVE)

Tammy Williams swinging by the sea (RIGHT)

Launching is a joint effort, Lower Bay (OPPOSITE)

If you are new here . . .

GETTING AROUND

Taxi is your best choice for a start. All taxis – whether minibus, landrover or car – carry a licence plate with an 'H' on it (for Hire). They congregate under the Almond Tree in Port Elizabeth and most monitor channel 68 on VHF radio, as do hotels, restaurants, and other land stations. If you plan to be out late, arrange early for your return transport. Rates are fixed to various destinations and for island tours – these usually last one or two hours.

Dollar bus is fun for the more adventurous traveller. These minibuses and jeeps ply Bequia's main 'highway' from under the Almond Tree to Paget Farm. If not full to overflowing they will stop whenever and wherever they are hailed so just raise your hand, hop in, and hold on. One of the people riding with you is probably the conductor, or 'footman', so let him know where you want to get off as he will somehow impart this information to the driver. Pay the driver as you disembark. Although sometimes hard to find at slack hours or at night, buses run frequently to coincide with the St Vincent ferry schedule. Check under the Almond Tree where they linger waiting for a full load.

The ferryboat Admiral *seen from the road behind Gingerbread as it comes into the main jetty*

Water taxi is a useful and pleasant way to get around Admiralty Bay, Bequia's extensive harbour. Think of a snorkelling trip to Devil's Table, or a drop at Princess Margaret Beach or at Lower Bay. Water taxis are usually found at the Frangipani, Whaleboner, or Gingerbread jetty. Remember to arrange for the return pick-up.

Rental cars and motorbikes are possible but take into account that the roads are not like the ones you are used to. Take your international driver's licence to the Revenue Office for a temporary St Vincent licence. If you have no international licence there will be a fee to pay for the local licence.

Mountain bikes, with these hills, are obviously for the fit. Rental is in Port Elizabeth opposite the dinghy dock.

Now back to work; the rain has stopped

On foot is still a fine way to see this island of a thousand views. Say hello to everyone you pass. It takes 35 minutes from the Harbour to Friendship Bay or Lower Bay, one hour to Industry Beach. Avoid the midday sun, and do not be surprised by the sudden darkness after 6.30 pm. For suggested walks and a map refer to page 75.

CLIMATE

Only a few degrees difference in temperature throughout the year ensures that Bequia seldom experiences over 90°F (32°C) or below 70°F (21°C). The dry season from January through to April happily coincides with the tourist season. Visitors are requested to conserve water at this time. The rainy season, usually in May and June, and again in October and November, rarely involves days of endless precipitation. More often a warm, torrential downpour will be followed immediately by a sudden outburst of sunlight.

Through most of the year Bequia basks under gentle cooling breezes but in December and January expect the Christmas Breeze – a strong, steady wind with accompanying higher seas. The opposite effect occurs during the latter part of August and September when Bequia passes briefly out of the tradewind belt.

Although Bequia is within the hurricane area, and ships must take care during July, August and September (meteorological offices give advance notice of weather disturbances from three days to a week before), there is not much likelihood of serious hurricanes in Bequia even during the hurricane season. Most pass well north of here and have not yet built up the force they display as they approach the North American mainland.

You may encounter certain phenomena of weather. A **ground swell** or **surging** is a condition of the sea reflecting weather some distance away. Breakers pound on the lee shore of the island (never the windward side) from Lower Bay to Hamilton, although waves are not noticeable out to sea. The *haze* which sometimes obstructs the clarity we normally expect may be due to Sahara Dust which surprisingly has made the journey across the Atlantic and goes on to affect as far west as Jamaica. There is also the possibility that this haze is the result of the volcanic eruption in the Philippines in 1991.

But normally in Bequia weather is decidedly a non-topic being so consistently beautiful as not to be worth mentioning.

The Bayshore Mall offers various shops and services, including a bank

CURRENCY

The Eastern Caribbean Dollar (EC$) used throughout St Vincent and the Grenadines is also the currency of Antigua, Dominica, Grenada, St Kitts and St Lucia. It is tied to the US Dollar (US$1.00 = EC$2.68). Hotels will usually change British pounds, Canadian dollars, and sometimes French francs and Deutschmarks. There are three banks in Port Elizabeth, open Monday to Friday from 8.00 am to 1.00 pm with additional opening on Friday from 3.00 pm to 5.00 pm. You will need a passport or driver's licence to change traveller's cheques. Most businesses accept US$ traveller's cheques and major credit cards.

ELECTRICITY

Local current is 220 volts, 50 cycle. American appliances require a transformer. Most outlets are 3-pin, flat.

TELEPHONE AND FAX

St Vincent and the Grenadines has an excellent direct long-distance dialling system. Phone calls and fax may be transmitted at Frangipani Yacht Services and at Gingerbread restaurant. You may purchase phone cards to use in public phone boxes, for example near the Tourist Bureau at the main jetty.

DRESS CODE

Most Bequians dress casually except for church services and for weddings and funerals. Ties, jackets, stockings and very high heels are rarely seen. Visitors when shopping or visiting government offices should never do so in just a swim suit or a brief sun outfit. Men are expected to wear shirts except on the

Almost everyone looks happy on the way to church

beach or on a boat. Nude and topless bathing are against the law.

MEDICAL

There is a small hospital/clinic in Port Elizabeth. The doctor resides nearby and holds a private clinic downstairs at home from 4 pm to 6 pm every day except Sunday. Public health services are largely free for Bequians. When visitors make use of facilities, donations to the Hospital Fund are appreciated. Serious cases may be referred to the General Hospital in Kingstown or to one of the private hospitals on the mainland.

POST OFFICE AND POLICE STATION

These are located side by side in Port Elizabeth opposite the main jetty. Police can extend your stay for a period of up to one month.

GOVERNMENT

Bequia is part of St Vincent and the Grenadines, an independent country within the British Commonwealth since 1979. The form of government is based on the Westminster system with representatives elected democratically in each of 15 constituencies, the Prime Minister being the representative who commands a majority of the other elected members in Parliament.

The present representative for the Northern Grenadines (Bequia and Mustique) is a native Bequian, the Right Honourable J F (Son) Mitchell. He is currently Prime Minister.

Elections are contested at least every five years and voter turnout is generally high at around 85 per cent.

The government selects a Governor General who acts as the Queen's representative, and whose function is largely ceremonial.

CHURCHES

The traditional churches in Bequia – the Anglican ones in Port Elizabeth and at Paget

St Mary's Anglican Church, Port Elizabeth, Father Ron Armstrong presiding

The Police Station and Post Office, Port Elizabeth

Farm, and the Roman Catholic one in Hamilton – have been joined in recent years by the Seventh Day Adventist Church in Port Elizabeth and Paget Farm, and various Baptist and Fundamentalist congregations.

92-year-old Mathilda Williams regularly rings the bell for service at St Michael's Roman Catholic Church, Hamilton (LEFT)

Father Gerry Farfan and acolytes processing for Sunday Mass. The church carries a cornerstone inscribed Dom AD 1927

EDUCATION

Primary school children may be seen decked out in their uniforms according to which of the four schools they attend. Two are government operated, one is run by the Seventh Day Adventists, and one, the Lower Bay School, is privately sponsored.

There are two secondary schools – the government-assisted Bequia Anglican High School and the Seventh Day Adventist Secondary School which are on opposite sides of the playing field behind Port Elizabeth. However, many Bequian children do not continue school beyond primary level.

A school for the handicapped, the Sunshine School, is supported largely by assistance from interested persons abroad with the principal teacher provided by the government.

Assembly at Paget Farm Government School (ABOVE)

Students of Bequia Anglican High School in the science lab (ABOVE RIGHT)

Chester Peters, Lawrence Rohomon and Geoff Wallace assisting at a Rotary Club cook-up (OPPOSITE)

SERVICE CLUBS

The Rotary Club of Bequia, which was officially chartered in 1988, has taken on many community projects such as Bequia Carnival, the hospital, and the building of water wells. A youth arm *Interact* was begun in 1992. Meetings are on Tuesdays at the Old Fig Tree.

The Bequia Sailing Club is probably the oldest service club in Bequia. Organised in 1981 on a non-profit basis by, among others, the present Prime Minister, the charter aims to encourage all types of sailing. Although the main annual event is the famous Bequia Easter Regatta (see page 92), other functions such as fishing boat races and coconut boat races give a lift to many holidays throughout the year.

History

The Amerindian Arawaks and, later, the more warlike Caribs were the first settlers that can be identified on Bequia. Pieces of their pottery are found on the shores of Admiralty Bay and on the windward coast at Park Bay.

In 1664 France laid claim to Bequia but did not establish settlements of a permanent nature. In 1675 a slave ship sank off the Bequia coast. The Africans who managed to swim ashore eventually mixed with the native Caribs to form the Black Caribs. Early travellers described the people they found as naked and, not surprisingly, hostile. In fact the fighting ability of the Caribs kept Europeans out of St Vincent and the Grenadines, while Britain, France and Spain fought over most of the rest of the Caribbean. In a treaty of 1660 the French and English actually agreed to leave the Caribs on the islands of St Vincent and Dominica undisturbed which indicates the difficulty the Europeans encountered in conquering these proud people.

Between 1719 and 1763 French settlers set up lime, indigo and sugar factories in Bequia. But by a treaty between the French and English in 1763 St Vincent and the Grenadines was designated British. Nevertheless concessions must have been made to existing French settlers as (in his map and survey of 1776) John Byers, under the direction of the Commissioners for the Sale of Lands in the Ceded Islands, marks those allotments which had previously been made by the

Carib pottery found in Bequia including the triangular foot of a three-footed griddle, the black painted side of a cooking pot, a lizard-like face which was probably a handle, and a human face with a surprised expression

14

A traditional Bequia house, two storeys with peak roof supporting a shed roof to the side, sash and louvre windows, and gingerbread trim

French Governor of the Windward Islands to Frenchmen with names like Gelleneau, Brocette and Labord. He also allocated 'for the defence of the Island certain pieces of Land intended to be appropriated for Forts, Batteries and such Military and Naval purposes as may hereafter be found most expedient and necessary.' Cannon and ruins have been found on several of these sites.

Two of the choicest agricultural valleys, Friendship and Hope, were set aside for the chief Commissioner, Sir William Young, formerly governor of Dominica. Two smaller portions were marked for Warner who apparently was Charles John Warner, grandson of Sir Thomas Warner, the Governor of St Kitts. His father had been the product of a liaison between Sir Thomas and a Carib woman of Dominica. Gravestones found at Paradise on the hill above the harbour bear the Warner name. Twenty smaller lots were cut out 'to be appropriated for the use of poor settlers'. The island, now mainly in English hands, began to cultivate cotton and then sugar.

The lucrative new crop of sugar was causing an economic and social revolution in the Caribbean. Small landholdings were giving way to large plantations and the resultant rise of a wealthy planter class. From the Spanish these planters soon learned the efficacy of slave labour which could be secured in Africa in comparison to the working class English and Irish lads who had come to the islands for adventure, or who even were dissidents sent away from home as punishment. Slaves were less unruly, worked better in the sun and were cheaper.

But the introduction of slave labour put thousands of non-propertied whites out of a job. With no money to return home they drifted to other islands in the chain. It was thus that some of them came from Barbados to Bequia and settled in the hills of Mount Pleasant. To this day the native Bequian whites are sometimes referred to by locals as 'Bajans'.

In the 1860s a Frenchman, Joseph Ollivierre, received a grant from the British consul in Jamaica for 70 acres of land at La Pompe in Bequia. Ollivierre is now the most common family name on the island.

From Scotland came William Thomas Wallace whose son, William Thomas Jr, introduced whaling to Bequia. Having worked on one of the New England whaling ships that came to the Caribbean chasing the humpback whale, Bill Wallace started his own shore whale fishery in the mid 1870s out of Friendship Bay. The Ollivierres followed suit in 1876 with a fishery at Petit Nevis.

Whale-meat was a staple food for the population in those days of relative poverty and before imports and deep freezers. Whale-meat could be 'doved' (cooked up in its own blubber) to be eaten immediately, or packed in containers and preserved by a covering of its own oil. Some was 'corned' – salted and dried for later use. The blubber was utilised for cooking oil and fuel in lamps.

Today only one small whale fishery exists. Athneal Ollivierre, the chief harpooner, leads a crew of six in his 26-foot traditional double-ended whale boat *Why Ask*. The design is based on that of the small boats carried aboard the American mother ships which roved the world before the turn of the century from the Artic to the Caribbean searching for the mighty whale. With a

Friendship Bay looking south towards La Pompe and the islands of Petit Nevis and Isle à Quatre

rugged design that could take all weather conditions this became the prototype for the standard fishing boat of the Grenadines, whereas on the mainland of St Vincent and north it is the Carib hollowed-out-log canoe which set the fishing boat style. These types of boats can be compared in a display set up by the Bequia Museum Committee in Port Elizabeth near the market on the bayside.

There is great excitement in Bequia on the rare occasions when a whale is secured. Groups gather on the hills to follow the hunt with cries of 'Blows, man, blows!' Butchering

Harpooner and chief whalerman Athneal Ollivierre in the last whaleboat, Why Ask
(NATALIE WARD, LEFT)

An old photograph of Port Elizabeth showing a schooner and a crowd of people at the jetty and several schooners in the background, one being careened. On the left the public convenience was built out on stilts over the water

is done on the off-shore island of Petit Nevis with a constant traffic of small boats ferrying men, women and children across the short channel to marvel at the whale's size, to observe the cutting up, to claim their share, and to cook or salt-down some on the spot.

Other economic activities in Bequia's past include burning coral to produce the lime used in building, much as we now use cement, and the processing of indigo for dyeing cloth. The indigo plant still grows wild on the island, and the remains of the stone vats used to soak the leaves and branches before extracting the dye can be seen at Park and at Anse-le-Coite. Cotton and sugar were Bequia's principal crops but cocoa and rum were also exported.

Excursions from St Vincent arrive at the main jetty, Port Elizabeth

This picture of a little house in the harbour was taken around 1960. It has since been demolished. Notice the pretty balustrade and the pieces of gingerbread used for decoration. Some rocks on the roof presumably hold down the galvanised, and an old oil drum collects the important water run-off (MACPHUS SARGEANT, BELOW)

Queen Elizabeth, accompanied by Prince Philip, plants a flamboyant tree in the town named after her, during her visit in 1985 (BELOW)

The Iron Duke, *now over 100 years old and many times rebuilt, is the original Bequia whaleboat purchased from an American whaling ship* (ABOVE)

In 1936 the burghers of Bequia's main settlement at the head of Admiralty Bay decided to grace their village, until then known simply as 'The Harbour', with the name 'Port Elizabeth' after the young British princess. King George VI soon gave retroactive approval but it was not until October 1985 that Elizabeth, now Queen, paid her first visit. Two commemorative flamboyant trees were planted by Her Majesty and Prince Philip, and are flourishing in the gardens near the small jetty.

Dependent on the sea for much of their food and for all of their communication with the outside world, Bequians had to become boat-builders. After the decline of the planter economy following the emancipation of slaves in 1834, there was a surge of sea-related activities – whaling, fishing, trading through the islands. Boat-building was the essential skill without which none of these would have been possible.

When the Bequians began to whale it was natural for them to copy the style of the small boat they had seen aboard the large whaling ships which sometimes passed into Bequia. One of these, the *Iron Duke*, was purchased from an American whaling ship by Bill Wallace when he set up his shore whale fishery in 1875. Now, having been rebuilt many times, the *Iron Duke* is still doing service as a seine boat out of Lower Bay.

From the 1840s until very recently almost all the regional trade in the Eastern Caribbean was carried on by boats built either in Carriacou or Bequia. Doug Pyle in his book *Clean Sweet Wind* accounts for 83 schooners built in St Vincent and the Grenadines in the forty peak years from 1920 to 1960, most of these probably in Bequia. He notes the probable influence on the design of the Bequia schooner, over the years, by the Nova Scotia schooners which traded into Barbados.

But the original knowledge for the complicated production of a schooner came through the island of Canouan, twenty miles south of Bequia. It was here in 1838 that the island's English owner brought a British shipwright, Benjamin George Compton. His daughter married William (Bill) Mitchell from St Vincent who had come to Canouan to learn boat-building. The Compton–Mitchell influence was destined to pervade this important new occupation throughout the Eastern Caribbean. While his brother went to Dominica, Bill Mitchell migrated to Bequia. His son, Harry Mitchell, built many schooners, *Valkyrie, Agneta, Altenera, Coronna* and *Water Pearl*, to name a few.

In 1939 Harry's son, Reginald, launched the largest schooner ever to be registered in the lesser Antilles, the 165-foot, 178-ton *Gloria Colita*, which traded as far as South America, Cuba, and the United States. This was the ship that suffered a mysterious fate in the Bermuda Triangle where it was found drifting with no one on board.

The launching of the Gloria Colita *in 1939 on the beach beside what is now the Frangipani took over two weeks. Her great weight kept breaking the rollers and she was stuck in the sand for several days. This photo was probably taken at that time. People had come from all over Bequia to help to cook enormous quantities of food – a whole cow, goats, chickens, rice, peas and ground provisions – and to take advantage of the drinks offered to put spirit into the launchers.*
Men scrambled about shifting rollers and positioning jacks and tackles. Women were in the majority on the teams which pulled on the massive rope.
Old Tex from Ocar sat high on the slanting stern leading the singing of the sea shanties such as:

Heave her away, for my dear macamay*
Aye, yae, yae, heave her away.

(* godmother)
or

What should a white man eat for supper,
Mosquito leg and sandfly liver,
Blow, boy, blow.

When she found her depth and floated for the first time, a goatskin band of home-made drums, triangle and shak-shak burst into a frenzy of percussion, and the elated crowd danced on the then wide beach. (SIDNEY MACINTOSH)

Large container ships now bring most of the cargo to the islands, but many Bequia-built vessels are still in use. *Friendship Rose*, after 25 years of carrying passengers, mail and cargo, has been fitted-out to carry visitors to the Tobago Cays and Mustique on daytrips. Bequia vessels also carry cargoes of fish to the markets in Martinique.

Currently, Orbin Ollivierre, a descendant of the Compton–Mitchell boat-builders, is finishing a 40-foot fishing trawler at the same site where his father Haakon Mitchell brought several vessels to life. This is the first boat he has worked on which is not intended to carry sail, although motor vessels have been built on the island before – notably the 102-foot *Wallace Triumph* launched from Lower Bay in 1964.

Friendship Rose, *formerly Bequia's faithful ferryboat, has now been remodelled into a tourist carrier for day charters*

The Wallace Triumph *launched in Lower Bay in 1964 was, at over 100 feet, the largest power boat ever constructed in Bequia. Owned by the three Wallace brothers – Curtis, Dawson and Henry – she was built under the supervision of chief carpenter, Ernest Adams*

Many a yacht needing repairs or a refit has blessed the skills of the Bequia shipwrights and sailmakers who make a stop in Bequia useful as well as enjoyable.

For many years Bequia men earned a good living on huge freighters sailing the oceans of the world as merchant seamen. Unfortunately this employment has been reduced drastically in the past few years.

Bequians now look for their livelihood to lobster diving, fishing and tourism with the first two dependent to a great extent on the latter. Large hotels have not, so far, been tempted to invest in this small island with a severe shortage of water, but small hotels, guest houses and rental properties have done much to raise the standard of living. Yacht visitors and cruise ships also make their contribution in port dues, passenger fees, and purchases of goods and services.

Orbin Ollivierre building his fishing trawler at St Hillary on Friendship Bay

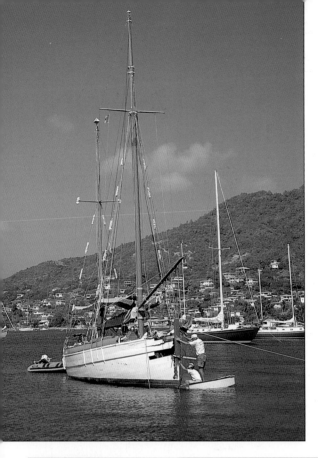

The new Bequia airport, christened the J F Mitchell Airport on 15 May 1992, brings visitors on extended holidays and for day trips from nieghbouring islands such as Barbados and Martinique.

Over the years Bequia has managed to retain much of her charm in spite of, or perhaps because of, her development. A felicitous mix of local, partially local, and foreign businesses has allowed her to hold fast to her character while becoming increasingly sophisticated. To keep this happy balance will be the interesting challenge of the future.

Admiralty Bay is ideal for making repairs (LEFT)

Ornie Ollivierre is happy to entertain visitors on the boat he is building on Athneal Ollivierre Beach

Son of Bequia, Prime Minister

James Fitzallen (Son) Mitchell, Prime Minister of St Vincent and the Grenadines, is Bequia's best-known personality. Born in the family home in Belmont (now the Frangipani Hotel) to a young Mount Pleasant girl who had married a charismatic sea captain from the Harbour with family connections in La Pompe and Paget Farm, he has the political advantage of being related to almost everyone on the island. He remembers as a child that when his father's schooner appeared around the point after a long sea voyage the beach would quickly be lined with Bequia folk hastening to greet him, many carrying a bowl or tin for the rice he never failed to bring back to share out.

His family had assets in land and ships but Son Mitchell had a typical Bequia childhood for the time – plenty of fish and mangoes, but a limited supply of just about everything else. It was not butter and jam he was accustomed to on his bread, but butter *or* jam. A regimen of church attendance was imposed and for several years he served as an acolyte in the Anglican church.

At the age of nine he experienced the shock of his father's disappearance at sea. The largest schooner ever built in Bequia, the *Gloria Colita* (named after Son's sister), was found with decks awash, sails only half down, in the Bermuda Triangle, with not a soul on board. The trauma was exacerbated by endless public speculation about what really had happened. This was during the war and some said Reggie had been captured by the Germans, others thought he had gone over to the Germans and was helping them pilot ships in the region. It seemed uncanny that before leaving South America for that last fateful voyage his eight Bequia crew had opted to leave the ship and return so that Reggie, who was fluent in several languages, had hired an all Spanish crew in their stead.

Two years later Son's mother remarried and moved to St Lucia with her three younger children leaving Son to continue the education he had just begun at secondary school on the

mainland of St Vincent. The resulting separation from both his family and from Bequia must have been a toughening ordeal and may explain the dogged tenacity which he subsequently displayed during various difficult periods of his political career.

Getting started was no easy task. Son's attempt to form a new political party, the GCUM (Grand Caribbean Unity Movement) whose main tenet was Caribbean unity, was not appreciated by the established parties. At his first public meeting in Kingstown's market square he was heckled mercilessly by party toughs and even stoned. To run for a seat in the Grenadines he had to beat the sitting member of twenty years, Clive Tannis, and his own uncle, Cyril Mitchell, who at first refused to give him his support.

An excellent and thorough campaigner, however, he won the seat and became Minister of Agriculture in a Labour Party Government for which his education at the Imperial College of Tropical Agriculture in Trinidad had prepared him well.

Prime Minister Mitchell in a serious moment of his speech at the rededication of the Friendship Rose. *Owners Henry Adams (left foreground) and Calvin Lewis (standing on the opposite side of the boom) listen intently, as do their families and other well-wishers*

But after several years, feeling that the government was not doing enough for the Grenadines, he resigned to stand as an independent candidate. In the ensuing election the other two parties won six seats each and Son was able to form a coalition with Ebenezer Joshua, leader of the People's Political Party. Son took for himself, of course, the position of Premier.

Resented by the majority of the people of the mainland as a usurper, being called scathingly 'the Bequia fisherman' and, having to work with a man who had himself already been head of government, this was not a happy time. When, after two years, the coalition collapsed Son boldly put someone else to run for him in the Grenadines, and he ran for a seat on the mainland. He lost both the government and the St Vincent seat; he had gambled himself out of a place in Parliament.

The distress amongst the people of the Grenadines was intense. There was an ill-fated uprising by some young men in Union Island which was quickly put down. A state of emergency was declared which meant the government of the day was able to postpone the by-election in the Grenadines which would later give Son back his seat.

Politically this was probably Son's lowest point. From here he began to build a new political party concentrating on securing grass roots' support on the mainland which was the essential basis for a credible national party. The Grenadines, he knew, would support him whatever he did. At the next election, much to the surprise of many, the New Democratic Party won the day and, as St Vincent was by now an independent state, Son became, for the first time, Prime Minister.

Moving from strength to strength his party won all fifteen seats in the election of 1989. It is an indication of Son's campaigning acumen that he predicted (although he did not make public) not only his victory in every seat, but also, with 100 per cent accuracy, which of the few polling stations he would lose in each constituency.

Other than winning elections Son's greatest talent has probably been the ability to get things done. The Bequia Airport is a good example of a large project he achieved by tenacious lobbying over many years both of potential donor countries and of the Caribbean governments in the region whose support was necessary to qualify for funding.

Son's place in history is assured. Time will tell whether his reputation will rest primarily on the many projects he has made possible, or whether he will be remembered more for what he has allowed *not* to happen in Bequia – land speculation, overdevelopment, and the potential dangers of economic exploitation.

The Land and
its creatures

AGRICULTURE

Unlike the mainland of St Vincent whose abundant rainfall and rich soil produce a huge variety of vegetables, Bequia has traditionally relied on three subsistence crops. As soon as the welcome rain has soaked the soil after the long dry season Bequia women are out in the 'ground' with their hoes preparing the land for corn, peas and cassava. The ripe corn will be roasted over a coalpot and the blackened kernels prised off individually to be eaten like a sweet, charcoal-grilled popcorn. Or it will be ground into meal for old favourites such as conkies (see recipe on page 58), 'coo coo' or 'fungie'.

Pigeon peas, green or dried for storage, make a wonderful soup, as well as providing one of the essentials for the perennial dish for special occasions, 'peas n' rice'.

Cassava too has a fantastic capacity for storage. One yachtsman sailed from Bequia leisurely around the world arriving back with his supply of 'farine', the meal made from cassava, in as perfect a condition as when he left, seven years previously. The *cassava* is stirred and baked over a fire in a huge iron cauldron or 'copper' in order to remove the poisonous hydrocyanic acid which, legend has it, the Caribs drank rather than face defeat by the British. Once processed the resulting 'farine' needs no further cooking but can be added to stews or broth for substance, or made into a delicious stuffing for fish.

Corn is planted by the roadside in Lower Bay
(LEFT)

Now a few garden vegetables are grown in Bequia, primarily *lettuce*, although this requires watering through the dry periods. Fortunately a good supply of fresh vegetables is available from the mainland of St Vincent and may be purchased at the market or from vendors.

TREE CROPS

Certain fruits grow better in Bequia than on the mainland. In the spring months *sapodillas* and *Bequia plums* are much in demand. *Limes, grapefruit* and other citrus fruit are plentiful in winter while summers are dominated by the *mango*. Try also the *cashew* fruit (pronounced 'coo shoo'), *guava, sugar apple*, the vitamin-rich *cherry, soursop* and *paw paw* (papaya).

Large flowering trees thrive in Bequia, their size rendering them unsusceptible to the seasonal drought to which many smaller plants succumb. *Flamboyant*, pink and yellow *cassia*, and *yellow poui* put on a spectacular show in the spring and summer months.

The calabash or boley is an inedible fruit with a hard shell which, when cut in half, scooped out and dried, makes a useful bowl or boat bailer

Harriet brings vegetables to sell in Bequia from St Vincent

NATURAL VEGETATION

The *white cedar* trees whose bent limbs have provided the ribs of many a Bequia vessel are the most prolific trees on the island. In April you will see their pale pink or white blossoms

Flowering trees: flamboyant
yellow poui
frangipani

The Adams garden, Belmont, euphorbia and poinsettia

In the shade of an almond tree at Hamilton

Hibiscus (TOP LEFT)
Ixora (CENTRE LEFT)
Seagrape (BOTTOM LEFT)

soft-coating the roads and drifting across the harbour. The **bay tree**, locally known as '**cinnamon**', is used to make an infusion for drinking. **Coconuts** abound. But beware on isolated beaches of the small-leafed tree with little green apples – that is **manchineel** – *not to be eaten*, or even touched (see photograph page 73). Look instead for the **seagrape** with leaves the size of your outstretched hand. These bear a pale mauve grape with a pleasant mild flavour. One of the most useful trees is the **wild almond** whose spreading limbs and large leaves provide many gathering places along the bayside.

CREATURES

There are a few harmless grass snakes on the island but the noise you hear in the undergrowth is invariably a ground *lizard*. These khaki coloured critters of up to a foot in length zig zag interminably through dry twigs and leaves making, it seems, as much racket as possible. Perhaps they aim to frighten other animals, not just tourists.

Similar in shape, but usually a brilliant lime green and with a dinosaur ridge down their backs, are the much quieter *iguanas* who will sit motionless for hours in the grass or on a tree branch. Including the long tail, they range from ten inches long to three feet or more.

Indoors you may encounter a *house lizard*, usually under five inches in length. Lizards are useful mosquito eaters and can change colour according to their surroundings, chameleon-like, from dark green to pale sand. You may see a male with a sack, or dewlap, inflated under his chin, a part of the sex ritual. The transparent wriggly ones that

This large (over four feet including tail) iguana has no problem climbing the mango tree whose rough bark he grasps with prehensile toes

Tortoise (ANTHONY BLUNDEN)

lurk behind pictures on the wall and only come out at night are **geckos** or wood slaves.

The **manicou**, a protected species, is an awkward rat-like *opossum*, brown and white and up to one and a half feet in length. Fortunately you are unlikely to run into one.

BIRDS

Over forty varieties of birds have been recorded in Bequia although not the endangered St Vincent parrot which inhabits the rain forests of the mainland and nowhere else in the world.

Bequia's most high profile bird is the **blackbird**, (Carib: 'grackel'), whose inescapable 'tweet tweet tweet' is said to be the exhortation 'Bequia sweet, sweet!' The male is stunning black, the female dull brown and its habitat is the hotel terrace, especially at breakfast time. Hold on to your toast!

Also very common is the endearingly chubby, yellow-breasted **cecile** (bananaquit) which chirrups with great vigour for its diminutive four-inch size. These birds will perch on porch rail or chair, calmly surveying the scene or squabbling amongst themselves. Normally nesting in bushes they sometimes seek out an indoor location, such as a hanging lamp, messily but industriously importing strands of straw from outdoors for the purpose.

Similar in size and shape, but not colour, is the brown **grassquit**, a seed-eater which hops about from ground to bush to oscillating perch on a blade of tall grass.

The relatively large (10") grey and white **mockingbird** with its distinctive white-tipped fantail and melodious song will be seen everywhere. You may also spot the somewhat smaller **topknot**, (yellow-bellied *elaenia*) which has a noticeable double crest and a pale lemon-coloured breast. This particular flycatcher is only found in St Vincent and the Grenadines.

Hummingbirds

Booby bird

Also special to Bequia (known elsewhere only in Union Island and Tobago) is the **cocrico**, (rufous-vented chachalaca), a large (22") turkey-like bird whose raucous 'cocrico' can be heard in the woods above Industry and Park.

One of Bequia's most fascinating birds is the tiny (3½") **doctorbird**, (Antillean crested hummingbird) whose mainly black coat flashes an iridescent blue-green according to

vicinity. The common **ground dove** (6–7″) pokes along on the ground picking up small seeds, sometimes accompanied by the much taller, long-necked *zenaida dove* (11″).

The largest bird you will see is the **man o'war**, or **magnificent frigatebird**, with an incredible wingspan of up to eight feet. Batman black, although the young and females have a white breast, the man o'war soars high over Admiralty Bay spotting fish which, curiously, must be scooped up from the surface as this bird is unable to dive or land on the water. Its feathers are not waterproof and if soaked it would never get into the air again. A favourite trick is to harass a booby or a seagull into dropping their prey.

The streamlined **brown booby**, a dusky brown with white, and over two feet in length, is, by contrast, a great plunger disappearing below the surface sometimes for half a minute at a time.

Gulls and terns are common sights around the harbour. The plentiful grey and white **davybird** (laughing gull) is recognisable for its dark bill and feet, and for its distinctive call 'ha, ha, ha', whereas the **royal tern** is whiter with a bright orange bill. Both are splendid divers. The beautiful **tropicbird** is larger with 18-inch white streamers trailing behind its mainly white body.

When walking beside the sea look for the **little blue heron** (18″) which poses on its long legs on rocks or jetties awaiting a chance to secure small fish or crustaceans which live where the water meets the land. Strangely, considering its name, this bird is not blue – the adult is slate grey whilst the young bird is pure white with chartreuse legs. The latter should not be confused with the **cattle egret**, also snow white but with a yellow bill and found near grazing cows who stir up the insects it loves.

Look also for **sandpipers** and **turnstones** that forage in the seaweed at the water's edge.

how the light catches it. This incredible flying machine hovers then nosedives into the multiple long-throated blossoms which are no problem for its slender curved beak. You may be alerted of its presence by a subdued 'cheeup' and the click of wings as it takes off again at incredible speed.

Often you will hear a repetitive mournful, hollow cooing emanating from bush or woodland. This indicates that doves are in the

Fishing

'It's billions of dollars in the sea that the almighty God create', says Jeff Gregg of Paget Farm. Born in 1928, the eldest of ten children, he was taught 'seawork' by his father from the age of eight, from fish pot to bottom line to seinework to trawling. As he sits in his shop in the village he rhymes off almost fifty varieties of fish with names like roundhead cavalli, whitening, porgyfish and old wife. 'But', he regrets, 'youngsters today don't want to work.'

The European settlers who first came to Bequia had no conception of fishing as a commercial operation. They were planters interested in making their fortunes through sugar and other crops, and probably limited the fishing activities of their slaves to keep them dependent on the estate.

Jeff Gregg in his shop at Paget Farm

But Bequia proved difficult for agriculture. The combination of the long dry season, the shortage of flat land, the neglect of absentee owners and the emancipation of slaves in 1838 brought about its inevitable decline.

In the late 1800s this vacuum in the economy gave rise to the development of more viable maritime activities, such as ship building, trading throughout the islands, and whaling. The latter was an important factor in developing the skills of seamanship which made commercial fishing feasible. To whaling also goes credit for the design of the Bequia fishing boat, a modified version of the American-style whaling boat. Fast, efficient and strong, these small sailboats, in the days before engines, were the key to reaching better fishing grounds some distance from Bequia and, also important, to opening up the market for fish on the mainland, nine miles across the channel.

Ninety-six-year old Amelia Duncan remembers when you could buy a strap of fish with an assortment of redman, grunt, butterfish and doctorfish, for four cents. But mostly, she says, in those times people gave fish to one another. Albert Peniston, a fisherman from Hamilton, explained that when they wanted to sell fish they were obliged to carry it to Kingstown, where it fetched 20 cents a pound. Bequia people, he says, were too poor to buy fish. Often he would rise at 2.00 am in the 'fore day mornin' and, using a flambeau, dip up some ballahoo for bait, then head out for Ramier (Pigeon Island) to do some bottom-line fishing. There was, for many Bequians, 'no other how fa mek a dollar.'

In the later 1940s vessels from Martinique began to buy fish in Paget Farm for shipment to Martinique and then France. French law forbade the importation of certain types of fish in order to protect their own

Reynald Chambers fixing the seine net

fishermen, but demersals like snapper, grouper, hind and butterfish were allowed, thus encouraging the bottom-line fishermen of Paget Farm and the setting of fish pots.

In the 1960s this trade was taken over by Bequia vessels which anchor in Friendship Bay, off Petit Nevis, or in the Southern Grenadines, buying until they have a full load then transporting the lot to Martinique. The use of these locally-built and owned vessels, such as *Strangerman*, *Five Nails*, *Content 2* and *Racio*, greatly assists in the retention of Bequia's boat-building and navigational skills.

In 1990 the new Kingstown Fish Market opened on the mainland. Modern refrigeration facilities allow the purchase of almost all the fish brought by fishermen, a real boon to the Bequia seine fishermen who, after a good throw, might have upwards of 5000 pounds of fish to dispose of. The situation will be improved further on completion of the new fish market in Paget Farm, a joint project of the governments of St Vincent and Japan.

The growth of tourism in Bequia has greatly increased the market for fish on the

island. Most restaurants feature fresh fish and lobster, and individual Bequians working in the tourist industry can now afford to buy the fish they no longer have the time to catch.

METHODS

Bequians use five methods of fishing.

Handlining for snapper, redman, butter-fish etc. is done in the waters around nearby islands like Ramier. The nylon line, which has four or five smaller lines attached near the base, is baited with live bait and weighted to sink. The boat is either banked – kept in more or less one place – or allowed to drift with the tide. In Paget Farm, Bequia's largest fishing community, 85 per cent of households have at least one member engaged in this type of fishing. Most seine fishermen, while waiting on the schools of fish they seek, will keep occupied by doing some handlining.

Seineboat fishing involves more equipment and financial outlay. Dennis Bynoe of Paget Farm, one of the dozen or so seineboat owners on the island, estimates that a 26-foot boat plus nets costs about EC$ 75,000.

When look-outs on the hill 'see a colour passing', or when lobster divers report sighting a school, the seine boat heads out with its crew of seven along with three smaller boats each with at least two men. Some of these are divers for the underwater work, formerly a job done 'on bare wind' but now made easier with mask and snorkel and in some cases with scuba equipment. During the period around full moon millions of tiny 'fry' beat ashore, pursued by schools of robin, jacks, cavalli, salmon, and bonito. Occasionally the seine boat goes out at night by the light of the moon.

The 500-foot by 50-foot seine net carries floats along one long side, and weights along the other. The net is carefully played out of the boat in a huge circle. Then begins the hauling in. Those in the boats pull on the

Nathaniel Peters mending a fish trap on Lower Bay Beach

Fresh roast fish at a beach picnic, Isle à Quatre

floating top of the net; the divers pull the foot line, first making sure that there are sufficient fish inside to make it worthwhile. When a small neat circle has been formed, the bottom is lapped to trap the fish and the whole thing is staked out on the seabed with anchors. All this may take three or four hours.

If the fish are not sold immediately they may be left trapped in the net for two weeks or more, but then it becomes necessary to protect the catch from sharks and other large fish by encircling the seine net with a bigger-mesh trammel net.

Towing, (trolling or trawling) is the style of fishing favoured by the fishermen of Mount Pleasant and the Harbour, using speedboats with powerful engines. Carefully gauging the tide which has a bearing on the location and movement of the fish, the fishermen progress up and down the Bequia channel, and down beyond Western Cay, often following the birds who follow the small fish being chased by the larger fish – like bonito (tuna), kingfish and dolphin. A piece of floating log or wood is also a signal – fish tend to congregate around it.

Sylvanus Peters on the Japanese-built fishing trawler he bought from the St Vincent Government

Spearfishing with mask and snorkel is done most often for personal use. No Bequia picnic is complete without a bubbling fish broth laced with dumplings, and fire-roasted fish not long off the reef. Local fishermen, however, are not allowed to spear fish in certain specified conservation areas, and it is illegal for foreigners to spearfish anywhere.

Scuba diving for lobster and conch is one of the quickest ways for a fisherman to earn money, although strenuous and potentially dangerous. Usually three men work from a speedboat: one diving, one swimming on the surface and one following with the boat. Most divers are well trained but some disregard the rules and must be rushed to the nearest decompression chamber in Barbados.

The shallower waters around Mustique and in the Southern Grenadines are the best grounds for lobster and conch. Many Bequia fishermen camp for weeks at a time in the Cays, and sell to hotels there or to buyers in Union Island who fly these valuable *fruits de mer* to eager purchasers in Martinique and France. Lobster is out of season in summer.

EQUIPMENT

The type of equipment used in the Bequia fishing industry is changing. Most of the original-style sailboats have been modified to carry a small engine. Many Bequians have abandoned sail to build plywood, fibreglassed speedboats with powerful engines.

The carib-style canoes used by fishermen from the Mainland – long, narrow hollowed-out logs with a sharp prow – are very fast with the addition of a high horsepower motor. They catch kingfish and dolphin above Battowia and often pass into Bequia to sell to hotels and restaurants before returning home to St Vincent.

When throwing a sprat net to catch small fry for bait the side is gripped in the mouth freeing up both hands to wheel out the net in a circular motion

Two 40-foot fishing trawlers, designed by the Japanese, and sold by the Government of St Vincent to Bequians, have refrigeration on board which allows them to stay out for several days at a time. They also use fish-finding radar, special bait and light sticks on the line to attract the fish. The latter are essential to capture the highly prized swordfish. These boats land and store very large albacore tuna, dolphin and kingfish.

SUPPLY

Although there is no shortage of fish in Bequia, except in periods of adverse weather, fishermen are having to go further and further to find the quantities which were known in the past. There is clear evidence that lobster and conch stocks are dwindling. This is a world problem and, indeed, fishing boats from very distant countries have been apprehended fishing in local waters. The introduction of scuba, of fish-finding radar and other sophisticated equipment helps to increase the catch, but the price may be high.

The fishing industry is Bequia's largest employer, and is complementary to the other main source of income – tourism. It is not an easy life, however. Danger is never far away. It is difficult to make a lot of money. Most fishermen improve their standard of living by keeping goats, sheep and chickens, and by doing much of their own house-building and maintenance. Their wives plant peas, corn and cassava, and sew and help with the livestock. Many fishermen however, have ambitions to emigrate, or move into another field.

Without new technology fishing will not be attractive to young people. But new methods will necessitate the implementation of programmes for the maintenance of fish stocks. The closed season on lobster is a step in the right direction. Similar regulations on conch are becoming increasingly urgent to assure their survival.

All in a day's whaling

We met at dawn, as arranged, on Friendship Beach. I tried not to feel out of place – a woman amongst twelve whalermen. Athneal Ollivierre, the chief harpooner and venerated folk hero of Bequia, had, after all, agreed.

Friendship Bay, so familiar to me by day, looked surreal in the early light. It could have been an old black and white postcard of itself, slowly coming to life.

The two whaleboats presided darkly on the silvery beach. Quickly one, and then the next, was gripped and escorted smoothly the short distance to the water's edge. Two 400-pound piles of large round stones were transferred with care into the bellies of the boats, the ballast that would prevent them from rolling over when wind hit sail.

The rising sun tipped liquid gold now onto the moving surface of the still sombre sea as the whalers checked and stowed the essentials. Each of the sturdy 26-foot boats contained the following: mast, sprit, sails rolled up and extended lengthwise, four hooded harpoons, three lances, a wooden tub of meticulously coiled rope and the galvanised bucket to pour water over the rope when the harpooned whale takes off – otherwise it would burn up with the friction. This bucket would double also as a cooking vessel for the fish we would catch with our tow-line on the sail to Mustique.

Also carefully stowed were the twelve 'breakfast' pans containing the cooked food from home to sustain the whalers during a day which might consist of simply watching from the look-out or, should a whale be sighted, could demand supreme mental and physical exertion over many hours during the chase and the kill.

As I stood in the surf awkwardly protecting my camera and eyeing the four-foot high gunwales of the boat beside me I was somehow scrambled into *Why Ask* and we were off, sliding through the accepting sea in the cool morning air, followed by our sister ship *Dart*. Five powerful oars with the arms to

Young fishermen

41

Loading ballast into the whaleboat (NATALIE WARD)

match got us the 200 feet or so from shore where it was deemed safe to raise the mast and put up the sails – a main and a jib.

These boats can sail. Going off the wind, as they are when returning from Mustique, they can make up to nine knots. Strong and seaworthy, they are built by hand using the appropriately bent limbs of local white cedar for ribs. The bow-shaped stern, which accounts for their classification as double-enders, gives mobility and lessens the danger of being swamped.

Every fine day in the whaling season from February to April the whalers make this trip to the look-out in Mustique. A watch is also kept from high points in Bequia and Isle à Quatre with communication traditionally by means of mirrors flashed in the sun.

Within an hour and a half we were pulling the boats up on the beach in Mustique. Masts and canvas were down resting the length of the boats in readiness for a quick launch should a whale be sighted.

We trudged a short section of neatly concreted road, but where it turned inland to the houses of the rich and famous we peeled off up a grassy track to the top of a hill. I understood the choice of this site as a look-out. There was an almost 360 degree panoramic view of the waters around the island. Before us lay the Bequia–Mustique channel which, being relatively shallow (120 feet), is good hunting ground for the humpbacks that migrate yearly from the north-east coast of Canada and the United States to the warmer waters of the Caribbean to have their young.

For years these men and their ancestors have surveyed the same stretch of water, waiting mostly, their trained eyes straining to focus on that thrilling sight – a whale spouting or giving a rolling leap out of the water – calling out 'Blows, man blows!' or 'Breach', as the case might be, then racing pell-mell down the hill, quick-launching the boats, giving chase, gauging where the whale will surface next and endeavouring to get there under sail alone. Engines, of course, would be impossible as the sound would alert the whale. Silence is so important, in fact, that the handle of the galvanised bucket is carefully wound with twine to prevent rattling as the boat speeds along.

At the turn of the century there were five whale fisheries in Bequia, each with several whaleboats. Whaling was an important part of the economy in the days when getting supplies from abroad was difficult and before tourism had appeared as a saviour in the employment situation.

But it was risky work then, as it is now. A lash of that giant tail can overturn or swamp the boat. When the whale is harpooned it may dive to the bottom carrying the attached boat with it, should the line not be fed out rapidly enough. Or it may take off at breakneck speed towing the whaleboat in a 'Nantucket sleighride', an incredible experience known to most of these men. As Athneal told me, 'If you want to catch whale you must be ready to go for a ride.'

When the whale tires, and the harpooner gets close enough to make the final thrust with the lance, (only Athneal has done this in recent years), someone has to clamber on to the whale's head and sew up the mouth with loops of rope to keep the jaw closed. Otherwise incoming water sinks the whale to the bottom where it is almost impossible to retrieve.

Towing the 40–60 foot hulk to shore for processing is a considerable feat. Previously the two whaleboats under sailpower alone might take hours to reach the Ollivierre's whaling station on the offshore island of Petit Nevis. A celebratory drink and the singing of whale shanties helped pass the time. Nowadays Bequia boats with engines are called upon to assist in the towing.

Winched up on a ramp on the bayside the whale is cut up ('flensed') and shared – a set portion to each whaler, to the boat owners, to the owners of Petit Nevis and to anyone else who contributed to the catch. These in turn give to their families and sell the balance to the many Bequians and other islanders clamouring for their piece of whale. There is no waste. Almost every portion of the whale is useful for food or to make a medicinal oil.

The men amused themselves on the hilltop. While some kept the look-out, others told yarns, teased one another, and cooked up a little fish broth. The sun got hotter. The sea was stubbornly devoid of any sign of life. A piece of lumber as a bench and a few coconut branches rigged up as sunshade were the only concessions to comfort. Perhaps men accustomed to perching on the gunwales of ships in all kinds of seas scorned anything more amenable on this dry hillside.

Some dozed off now and then giving the others the chance to play a favourite trick, attaching a piece of twine from the sleeper's clothing to a nearby post then shouting 'Blows, man, blows!' and laughing like crazy when he leapt up to take off down the hill, only to find himself attached.

I supposed fathers and uncles before them had joked in the same way, on this very spot. But for how much longer? I tried to imagine the young men of Bequia having the patience

Athneal in the whaleboat (NATALIE WARD)

for this type of life, or the courage. One can appreciate the time-frame that supported this method of hunting whale, but it is hard to reconcile this long-honoured method with the pace of life today. To turn to modern factory methods, however, would be unthinkable, given the danger of depleting the world whale population, and the force of environmental opinion.

Yet if this indigenous whaling dies out much else goes with it – the efficient use of a working sailing vessel, for example, – even the very existence of these graceful, self-sufficient whaleboats. On the human side, the brave skills and the underlying steadfastness of intent bred in the whalermen will no longer be required. The greatest loss will be the closeness to nature fostered by the necessarily intimate relationship between whale, sea and whalerman. These are aspects of Bequia that have been part of the environment for many years.

I was meditating thus, perhaps dozing off a little myself, when I heard the long-awaited cry, 'Blows, man, blows!' I leapt up to scan the horizon. Couldn't. My belt was attached to the bench. Hoots of laughter all round!

Alone now on Friendship Beach

At 2.00 pm, without the need for an order because this was the daily routine, the whalers gathered up the few items they had brought up the hill including our cooking pot cum rope cooler and, dry and hot, we made our way back to the beached boats and the waiting channel.

The disappointment I felt that I had not experienced chasing a whale was eased by a sense of relief at possible danger averted.

I then proceeded, unwittingly, to put myself more at risk than I had been all day. I accepted a ride back to Bequia with some friends who had a power boat – the usual 40-foot white hulk, with a noisy set of engines.

We were approaching Friendship Bay, but still to windward of Semples Cay, the rocky islet that stands guard at the entrance to the harbour, when the steering cut. Round and round we went in crazy circles. We shut off the engines, and drifted.

I soon realised that wind and tide were delivering us straight into the cay. Jagged rocks and smashing surf, in repeated violent confrontation, loomed closer and closer. I imagined armies of black sea urchins bristling in those crevices.

Why Ask and *Dart* were coming up now towards Friendship Bay, tough canvas curving taut in the wind. How I wished to be there, not here!

Realising our problem they threw us a line, and the two whaleboats, with the strength of the power in those sails alone, towed us, like a whale they had conquered, and deposited us safely at anchorage. With incredible poise and skill Athneal and his men had secured a deranged vessel from what appeared to be almost certain shipwreck.

It is doubtful if the Moby Dick style of Bequia whaling will endure past this generation. Future opportunities are more likely to be in the new field of 'whalewatching', now so popular in New England. It would be a fitting tribute to Athneal and his predecessors if a way could be found to use the traditional Bequia boats and the accompanying skills required to build and sail them.

Places of interest

There are wonderful views from all over Bequia. Of particular note are those from Cinnamon Garden, from the Fort above Hamilton, and from Mount Pleasant.

'Under the Almond Tree', also known as the 'House of Parliament', designates the shady outdoor gathering place of Port Elizabeth. Here, on benches encircling three ancient knobbed trees Bequians mix gossip, or 'commesse', with politics and business in the animated discussions with which they while away the time.

Of historical interest are the fort at Hamilton – little of the original structure remains but the French cannons found on the site have been remounted – and the Old Sugar Factory at Spring which is a picturesque mix of broken-down stone rubble walls and encroaching vegetation.

St Vincent from Cinnamon Garden

From Hamilton Fort looking towards Princess Margaret Beach and Lower Bay

Western Cay, also from the fort

There is a 'Whaling and Sailing Museum' proposed for a site at Friendship Bay but in the meantime a temporary exhibit of seacraft of the region has been mounted near the market in Port Elizabeth. If you are interested in the whaling culture of Bequia you can visit the whaling station on Petit Nevis, a 15-minute ride in an open speedboat from Friendship Bay or Paget Farm. You'll see the ramp where the whale is pulled up and the cauldrons where the blubber is rendered into oil. Or think of visiting Athneal Ollivierre who has his own display of whaling implements at his home at La Pompe.

Many visitors enjoy dropping in on one of the two model boat building 'factories', Sargeant's or Mauvin's. Starting with a piece of soft 'gumwood' or balsa these young men carve the hulls of whaleboats, local schooners and yachts on a miniature scale from one foot to four feet in length. With great accuracy they add the superstructure using colourful hardwoods which they varnish or paint in brilliant Caribbean colours. If you are tempted to buy one they will derig the sails and masts and pack your vessel in a handy box to take home.

Screen printing was introduced into the island thirty years ago by Linda Lewis, an American who set up the Crabhole Boutique. Fabric is sold by the yard or in ready-made clothes produced by Bequia women to the Crabhole's high standards.

Miniature newly painted rudders drying beside some finished models (ABOVE)

Sargeant's model boat shop, Hamilton (LEFT)

Another American, Tom Johnston, has made his mark at Moonhole which is a natural arch, over a hundred feet in height, through the point of land that narrows down toward Western Cay. He bought the land 30 years ago and he and his wife Gladys started the Moonhole Company, a private development of over twenty homes. One stipulation for would-be residents is that Tom must design your house for you. It is sure to contain no straight lines, and to incorporate existing features of the environment. Trees, cliffs, and in one case a functioning blow-hole through which the sea explodes every few minutes, are all happily part of his plans.

Tom Johnston

House at Moonhole

Accommodation

Half a dozen hotels have been the centre of accommodation for visitors for several years, along with a few thriving guest houses and, more recently, rental apartments and houses.

Historically the *Sunny Caribbee* (now called *Plantation House*) is the oldest. In 1946 the McIntoshes, a Bequia family of Scottish extraction, decided to take advantage of the nascent tourism to construct a graceful hotel, designed by Vincentian surveyor Charles Richardson, on what had previously been a sugar-cane field. For lumber they sawed some enormous logs which had washed ashore at Hope Bay after the U-boat sinking of a vessel carrying a deck cargo of timber from Africa.

Plantation House

Brian Collier has been cooking steaks for 14 years

Stone was secured from a broken-down sugar mill at Spring.

For many years this was Bequia's only hotel. It passed to the Tannis family of Bequia, and subsequently into European ownership. Prefab hardwood cabanas from Suriname were added on the well-tended grounds. Sadly the main building was razed by fire in 1988. The present replacement was modelled to some extent on the original.

In 1962 Noel Agard of St Vincent built the *Friendship Bay Hotel*. The British Young brothers took over to be succeeded by the American Coast Guard captain (among other things), Niels Thomsen. In the central building the dining room has a stunning view of the bay; cottages extend up the hillside.

The *Frangipani Hotel* was created by Son and Pat Mitchell in 1966 when Son returned from England to embark on his political career. The high-peaked, shingle-sided house had been built half a century before by Son's father, the sea captain Reginald Mitchell, with family quarters upstairs and storage for ship's gear downstairs. With the help of architect Klaus Alverman an open-sided wood and stone bar was added on one side, and then the dining room on the other, followed by more guest rooms on the hillside above. From the beginning a policy of serving fresh local food has prevailed. The Thursday night barbecue has become an institution.

Julie's Guesthouse was founded in 1974 by Julian McIntosh, a Bequian building contractor, and his wife Isola, starting with ten rooms. Famous for hearty meals and good value the business has expanded to 19 rooms, each with private bath. The McIntoshs have now handed over management to their daughter Shawn.

Bequia Beach Club, a 10-room hotel on the middle of beautiful Friendship Bay, was built by Bruno Fink, a former German football coach who, while visiting St Vincent with his soccer team in 1981, took a day sail to Bequia and fell in love with it.

Mr and Mrs McVille John opened their popular Lower Bay guest house in 1982 naming it *Keegan's* after their son. There are now 11 rooms each with private bath, and there is a beachside restaurant and bar.

Staff at the Frangipani Hotel

Two of the staff pose at the Beach Bar, Friendship Bay Hotel

Some of the other guest houses, apartments and hotels are:

Blue Tropic
Gingerbread Apartments
Hibiscus Apartments
Lower Bay Guest House
The Old Fig Tree
The Old Fort
Village Apartments.

Food

Bequia offers a variety of good food, much of it locally produced.

Seafood is paramount. Most Bequians eat fish every day. Try a kingfish or a dolphin steak, the latter being dolphin the fish, not the mammal. The lobster in these waters is spiny lobster, or *langouste*, which has no claws. It is out of season in the summer months. Shrimp is regularly imported from the Caribbean coast of South America.

The enormous mounds of large pink-flanged shells you see in many beachside locations, such as in the Tobago Cays, are testimony to the popularity of conch, also

Conch shells left on the rocks after extraction of the edible creature inside, done by knocking a hole in the back of the shell to release the suction

known as 'lambi'. Each shell has a hole knocked in the back to release the rubbery animal which must be pounded (you 'pung' it) to render it tender enough to cook. Curried and stewed conch are common, but the real Bequia favourite is conch souse (see recipe on page 59).

Local knowledge imputes aphrodisiacal powers to all seafood but most especially to conch. A Bequia lad faced with a breach of promise case when he failed to appear at the altar explained his unintended involvement with the girl to the judge, 'But she gave me conch's water to drink!'

Local meat may be beef (a cow is killed for special occasions such as a wedding or at Christmas), lamb or goat, the latter called 'mutton'. The sheep and goats you see are mainly reared for their meat. If you cannot tell the difference between them (no woolly coat in this climate!) remember that on sheep the tails turn down, on goats they point up. In the dry season proprietors tend to let their animals loose to range in other people's gardens where tempting morsels of hibiscus await them, so that this time of year is known also as the 'leggo' season.

Vegetables come from the mainland of St Vincent, where the fertile soils and abundant rainfall produce more variety than on any other island in the Eastern Caribbean.

Fruits abound, but visitors accustomed to the choice in big countries should be aware that fruit has a season and grapefruit, for example, bears in the winter months, but is scarce in summer. Papaya ('paw paw') and banana are around, however, most of the year.

Theresa Byron runs a restaurant and bar in Lower Bay

West Indian specialities such as 'roti' – a meat, conch or chicken stew enfolded in an edible pastry envelope – or 'callaloo' – a delicious thick soup resembling spinach – can be obtained at many eating places. 'Pelau' – meat or chicken cooked up in one pot with the rice – is a favourite especially when feeding a crowd.

Many restaurants feature local foods, or variations thereof, but international fare is

Audrie and McKie's cafe is right on Lower Bay Beach

easily obtained for those who fancy a good steak or Italian or French style cooking. There is a choice of well over twenty restaurants in Bequia, most of which monitor channel 68 on the VHF if you wish to make reservations.

Recipes

AMELIA DUNCAN'S RECIPE FOR CONKIES

Young-looking ninety-six-year old Amelia Duncan sat in the café near the old coconut wharf, an area of Belmont that she has known, no doubt, longer than anyone else alive. She had dropped by to see me after walking, unassisted, from her home in Hamilton, a distance of at least half a mile. I asked her about the old days, about fishing, about the Mitchell's boat-building activities, and I was amazed, again, as always, that her mind was as clear and quick as ever.

Amelia Duncan

Born in 1898 she was given by her mother at the age of four to her godparents Harry Mitchell and his wife, 'Nen' Sarah (née Ollivierre), growing up in their homes at Hope, Belmont, and Isle à Quatre. The Mitchell's son was two years younger than her and when 'Capt'n Reg' married it was natural that she acted as nanny to his children. She was particularly close to his eldest, James or, as he would always be called, 'Son'. Amelia's devotion to the Mitchells was surpassed only by her faith in God and she long cherished the dream that 'Mr Son' would become a minister. The fact that he turned out to be a minister of government, not religion, was, no doubt, a satisfactory alternative.

There were many years when, for one reason or another, all her Mitchells were gone from Bequia. Amelia worked as a cook at the Anglican rectory, and then for the Sunny Caribbee (Plantation House) Hotel. When her beloved Son returned to enter politics in 1966 the Frangipani hotel was established in the Mitchell family home at Belmont. Amelia insisted on offering her services and she cooked there until she retired – her knowledge of local food and ways invaluable in the Frangi's early days.

Conkies, also known as 'dookana', are best made with local dried corn. The plantain leaves impart a waxy, gelatinous texture to the outside of the conkie. Open one of these parcels for breakfast and you are set for the day.

This is the kind of recipe useful in the days of Bequia's relative isolation, especially during the Second World War, when the imported wheat flour necessary for conventional bread and cakes was not always available.

Conkies

2½ cups dry grated corn (or cornmeal)
4 tablespoons margarine
½ cup grated sweet potato or pumpkin
1½ cups grated coconut
1½ cups sugar
1 ripe banana mashed
a few currants, nutmeg, cinnamon
few drops almond essence
(green plantain leaves or banana leaves to wrap)

Add a little water to the grated coconut and squeeze to make a thick milky coconut cream. Strain and discard the coconut.

Add the cream to the other ingredients. Mix to a thick dough. Cut the plantain leaves into six-inch squares. Put two tablespoons of the mixture on each, fold over each side into a parcel and tie. (Steam leaves to soften if necessary.)

Rest the parcels on a few sticks in a pan covered with two inches of boiling water. Cover and steam to cook for one hour frequently adding more water to prevent from drying out.

Serve warm, or chilled.

Conch Souse

as explained by Cosmos Simmons of De Reef Restaurant *and* Daphne Grant of Daphne Cooks It

Conch
Lime
Chilli pepper
Cucumbers
Sweet peppers
Onions
Salt and pepper

After 'pungin' the conch put them into a pressure cooker covered with water and scald for 5 to 10 minutes. Pour off this water which can be used, with a squeeze of lime, as a nourishing drink purportedly high in calcium and certain other exotic qualities, and much prized as a chaser in local rum shops.

Recover the conch with water and pressure cook for 20 minutes or so. Lift out the conch and chop small. Make a sauce out of the water they were cooked in by adding the juice of half a lime for each cup, plus a few sliced cucumbers, sweet peppers and onions, and salt and pepper. Slice finely a small portion of hot chilli pepper and add, to taste, but at least so you know it's there. Put back the conch in the sauce and serve in a soup bowl, warm or at room temperature.

Beaches

'Life's a beach', or can certainly seem so on those early-darkening wintry days to which most northerners regularly resign themselves. In Bequia there are beaches to choose from – warm, sparkling, uncrowded and accessible – no such thing as a private beach here; everything below high water mark is property of the 'Crown', ie the Government.

MAJOR BEACHES

There are five major beaches.

Tony Gibbons is also known as Princess Margaret Beach since she took a dip here off the Royal Yacht on her honeymoon. The name 'Tony Gibbons' remains, long after the person has been lost from local memory. This lovely curve of pure sand is generally calm except on the few occasions when there is a ground swell (see climate on page 7). An idyllic cove at the southern end entices you through a natural arch of rock. Go.

Some visitors venture to go topless on this stretch of sand but, as this is taboo amongst Bequians, please use discretion. There is a road to Tony Gibbons but a water taxi is better, or enjoy the six-minute hike over the hill from Plantation House.

Lower Bay, the longest beach on the island, is generally calm with beautiful sand and swimming. A short reef encloses a por-tion of the shoreline making a natural warm-water pool, excellent for children. Avoid the poisonous machineel trees along the shore (small leaves, little green apples – see photograph on page 73). Towards the south you see nets being mended and boats repaired for the village of Lower Bay, all but hidden on the flatland beneath the surrounding hills. Refreshments are available at De Reef, a gathering place especially on Sunday afternoons, as well as at Keegan's and at Theresa's. There is pleasant snorkelling from the southern tip of the beach along the land towards the west. To get to Lower Bay take the road which passes right beside the beach or arrive by water taxi.

Sea urchins, also known as sea eggs
Beware *– very painful when touched. Rarely in sand, they are a menace on rocks and coral*

Lower Bay Beach

Princess Margaret Beach

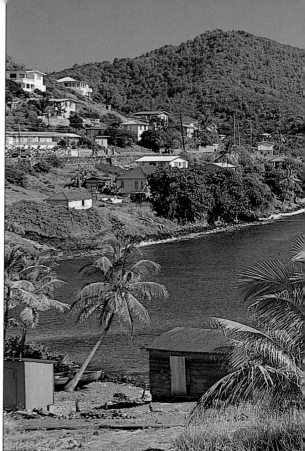

Friendship Bay, a long arc of sand on the eastern side of Bequia, is protected from the Atlantic by St Hillary Point. In the distance you see Mustique and, to the south, Petit Nevis. Swimming is good, often with gentle waves breaking. There is good snorkelling at the northern end. You will see brightly painted fishing boats pulled up on the southern section including, in whaling season, the last remaining whaleboat, *Why Ask*. The easiest access to this beach is by the road at the northern end.

This looks like a good spot (ABOVE)

Friendship Bay from La Pompe (ABOVE CENTRE)

In the surf, Hope Beach (RIGHT)

Hope, a horseshoe-shaped bay directly exposed to the winds of the Atlantic, is the most deserted beach on the island. Swimming in the surf is great fun, diving under huge waves to bob up and down in the relative calm beyond the point where they break, then riding them the short distance in to the sandy shore. Please, however, do not attempt to swim here unless you are experienced and with others. There is no snorkelling. The road is poor but you can get a taxi to the top of the hill and walk down. Carry something to drink.

Industry, also known as Crescent Beach, was named after sugar, once the thriving industry on this part of the island. Now the area is predominently farmed in coconuts and as pastureland. You will enjoy the steady breeze off the Atlantic but do not expect surf – there is a protective reef across the whole mouth of the bay. Snorkelling can be interesting (see sports on page 67). Access by car is easy; otherwise, opt for a good hour's walk from the harbour through flower-bordered coconut groves and past the tumbledown remains of the sugar factory at Spring. Drinks and lunch are available at the Crescent Beach Inn.

OTHER BEACHES

Other beach possibilities exist.

Park, which is beyond Industry, is coral encrusted and blustery. It is not good for swimming but makes an interesting visit none the less.

Ravine is difficult to reach but there is a dark sand beach. Do take care swimming here, however. In the rocks on the southern shore there is a fascinating blow-hole which spouts a huge plume of water every few minutes. If you look carefully on the northern rocky coast you will find a hole where the ebb and flow of the tide under the rocks rattles around a crop of smooth 'pebbles' of up to six inches in diameter.

Athneal Ollivierre Beach was named in 1992 after Bequia's foremost whaler. This stretch of sand was largely created by the huge sandsucking machine that was brought from the Netherlands to do the landfill for the adjoining airport.

Industry Beach, Balliceaux and Battowia in the distance (WILFRED DEDERER)

L'An Chemise (anse de chemin) is made up of many-coloured cobblestones. There is very good snorkelling. This beach is very difficult to get to by land as the path is usually quite overgrown, but can be reached by boat unless seas are rough.

Spring Beach through the coconut grove below Spring Hotel is a pretty bay but some may find it rather shallow for swimming.

Several ways to go to sea

A PRECAUTIONARY NOTE . . .

Visitors are urged when 'beaching it' to avoid taking an over-
dose of sun. Sunblisters and a giddy head are not what you
came for. A hat, cover-up shirt, sunscreen and plenty of liquid
to drink are well worth the trouble.

Sports
More or less physical activity . . .

I suppose **basking in the sun** all day, idly trickling sand through your fingers, is your idea of an appropriate holiday sport. But just lift that lazy head a moment and take a look – if you can see through those cool mirror shades – across the dazzling blue of Admiralty Bay. Don't you love those glistening multicoloured sails skimming over the surface of the water, like dragonflies, at incredible speed?

Sailboarding is ideal in Bequia. Basil, of Paradise Windsurfing, can get you started. Take your first fifty falls in the lee of the land, then dare to circuit the yachts at anchor until, with experience, you head for the stiff breezes at the harbour mouth. Or try Friendship Bay

Windsurfers at Lower Bay

where the prevailing wind always brings you back to shore. Best leave the powerful tradewinds at Industry Beach and Adams for the experts. For now just think of windsurfing as an exhilarating way to get your body on (and in) the water.

You can't lie in the sun all day! There are some choice shady spots along the shore where you could catch up on your reading, or more indigenously, watch the boats come and go.

Boat-watching in Bequia, is a lot like people-watching. You see all kinds – neat, neglected, fast, stodgy, old, young – and there's a story behind every one. Some have come from half-way around the world; others started life right here. This sport can keep you amused indefinitely. Binoculars are a useful adjunct for the dedicated.

Come to think of it, why not try a little *boating* yourself? Hire a Sunfish at Sunsports (Gingerbread), or look for one of the 'Bequia dinghies' – *Handy Andy* in Port Elizabeth, the *Iron Duke* at Lower Bay, or *Jeff Gregg* at Paget Farm. These former working fishing boats are more often used for pleasure now. But the rig is tricky so you'll need a captain. Plan to get wet!

When you discover how sailing lifts the soul you may want to try a *day charter* on a yacht. An hour's sail gets you to Isle à Quatre, an uninhabited island where you will anchor (possibly the only boat there) off a sandy curve of beach between craggy rocks. Snorkelling in waist-high water around some submerged boulders is especially good for beginners. You could also try the nearby island of Petit Nevis where you can see the last remaining whale fishery with the ramp and the vats for rendering the oil. On the windward beach there is a charming natural pool.

The constant breeze but calm water of Admiralty Bay – ideal for Sunfish sailing

For sale, for sail

A longer, more envigorating sail (two to three hours from Admiralty Bay, one hour from Friendship) brings you to Mustique. The best-known beach is called Macaroni. For snorkelling sample the reef to the right of the main jetty. To the left are Basil's Bar and some boutiques.

Two or three-day charters give you more scope. Sail to the Tobago Cays, for example, or the small island of Mayreau. It is possible, however, to see the Lower Grenadines and return to Bequia the same day if you take a speed launch, or a catamaran like *Passion*. The schooner *Friendship Rose*, formerly Bequia's faithful ferryboat, offers a sail to the Cays, lunch, a snorkel, and a flight back to Bequia from Union Island, all in a day.

Shelling on the beach on the island of Petit Nevis, islands of Balliceaux and Battowia in the distance (ABOVE)

Term charters of a week or more open up to you the whole of the Grenadines, from Mustique to Petit St Vincent and even, if you like, Carriacou – Bequia's sister island which is the most northerly of the Grenadines belonging to Grenada. When choosing a boat for a longer charter consider, besides the price, the calibre of radio, engine, toilet and shower facilities, cooking arrangments and the degree of privacy aboard.

But there is another world much closer at hand – the incredible paradise of Bequia's underwater environment. **Snorkelling** is possible for everyone requiring only a little patience to get the hang of (like how about breathing through your mouth which is attached, remember, to a tube of fresh air, and not through your nose which is enclosed in an air-tight glass cage). Rent mask, fins and snorkel from a dive shop – they'll show you how to fit up. This inexpensive sport is one of the most rewarding. Wear a T-shirt if you plan to spend long hours with your back exposed to the sun. Beware of passing speedboats.

Doing some snorkelling at Moonhole, day charter boat Passion. *Anchored nearby, the sunsports dive boat has brought some scuba enthusiasts (OPPOSITE)*

Raising the sail on Friendship Rose *(BELOW)*

Some spots to try:
- from the Southwest end of Lower Bay along the coast to the West
- Rocky Bay and Devil's Table, best reached by water taxi
- between Industry and Park Bays. Enter the sea at the southern end of Park Bay, drifting with the current, which keeps you safely inside the reef, around the point to Industry Bay where you go ashore, walk back over the hill, and repeat the process. If the current is very strong remember to stay close to the reef which is on your left as this is stiller water than in the open sandy stretches closer to shore. You may prefer to do this the first time with guide Ricky Nichols of Crescent Beach Inn.

Scuba diving brings even more of the fabulous underwater world into your range.

Four excellent dive facilities on Bequia can help you take the plunge, two on Admiralty Bay – Sunsports and Dive Bequia – and two at Friendship – Dive Paradise and Bequia Beach Club. No great physical strength or agility is required, so long as you are over 14, in reasonably good health, and not asthmatic or pregnant. You can do it. Millions have done it before you – diving is the fastest growing sport in the world. When you see the fascinating, colourful, peaceful world down there you'll feel as if someone has just handed you a bonus in life. And incidently, the underwater scene is usually still brilliant when clouds and rain have dulled our world above.

There is an incredible underwater environment to discover around Bequia

Whammo! Cricket on the beach

Volleyball at Lower Bay. Notice the ***poisonous machineel trees*** *on the right*

Diving in Bequia is noted for the easy proximity of numerous dive sites, and for the variety of fish. Even on your first dive you may find yourself a novice in a school of zillions of silvery minnows, or the playmate of a gang of reef fish bobbing in and out of the corals, or a voyeur daring to peep into the craggy habitat of a shy lobster. For a short time you will be transported out of yourself and the world you know.

Scuba entry experience (resort) courses take one and a half hours of classroom time, half an hour of shallow water skills training, and then you embark, suitably accompanied, on your first dive. To become a certified diver under either the Paddi or Naui system takes five or six days.

Well, if I can't entice you into the sea, perhaps the land is your thing. ***Football***

(soccer) and **cricket** are the local passions. The refurbished playing field, named after former member of parliament Clive Tannis, is behind Port Elizabeth, but you will probably see some informal games materialising on the beach. For cricket the boys use a tennis ball, with often just the stump of a coconut branch for a bat.

And then there's **tennis**. Courts are at Plantation House, which has lights, at Gingerbread, Friendship Bay and Spring Hotel.

Hiking is a wonderful way to get to know Bequia. Remember the midday sun is hot and that it gets dark soon after 6.00 pm. Bequia's many scenic roads are obvious choices for the walker, particularly the ones less travelled. But you may discover some interesting paths and goat tracks.

Saturday morning tennis lesson at the Gingerbread court. Tutor: Bob Berlinghof

Marathon winners pose on the beach at Paget Farm

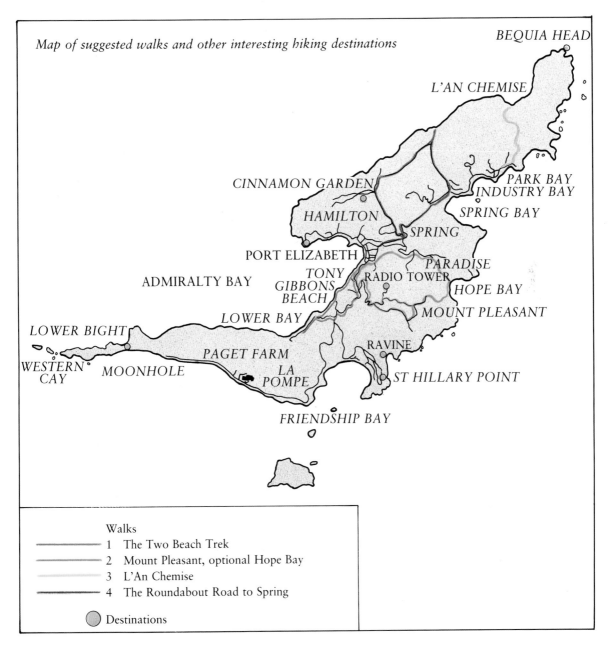

Map of suggested walks and other interesting hiking destinations

BEQUIA HEAD

L'AN CHEMISE

CINNAMON GARDEN

PARK BAY
INDUSTRY BAY
SPRING BAY

HAMILTON

SPRING

PORT ELIZABETH

PARADISE

ADMIRALTY BAY

TONY
GIBBONS
BEACH

RADIO TOWER

HOPE BAY

LOWER BAY

MOUNT PLEASANT

LOWER BIGHT

PAGET FARM

RAVINE

WESTERN
CAY

MOONHOLE

LA
POMPE

ST HILLARY POINT

FRIENDSHIP BAY

Walks
—————— 1 The Two Beach Trek
—————— 2 Mount Pleasant, optional Hope Bay
—————— 3 L'An Chemise
—————— 4 The Roundabout Road to Spring

⬤ Destinations

Here are some suggested routes.

1 The Two Beach Trek

30 minutes each way, fantastic value for effort

From the Plantation House Beach Bar it's a short distance along the bayside to the point of land ahead. The path over the hill is just beyond the rain gulley about ten feet in from the edge of the cliff. There are a couple of steep spots but it's not too far to the beautiful sweep of Tony Gibbons Beach, also called Princess Margaret Beach. Walk the full length of the sand and check out the romantic cove under the natural arch at the far end. Come back out to find the path by the trees at the top of the beach over the rocks. Where the path splits take the middle one to meet up

with the Lower Bay Road which you then follow down to a heady second dazzling beach of the day. At the far end, by the village of Lower Bay, fishermen mend nets and repair boats under the shade of the almond trees. Refreshments are available at several locations close to the beach. For variety going back keep to the road (instead of descending again to Tony Gibbons) curving inland up hill and down until you find yourself back in Port Elizabeth.

2 Mount Pleasant, optional Hope Bay

One hour each way, superb views, agreeable terrain except for the stony track to Hope. Take water to drink.

From Bequia's main highway south out of Port Elizabeth, a short distance past the Plantation House, the Mount Pleasant road cuts off sharply up to the left. Follow it left,

right, then left again, as you work your way up Belmont Hill under overhanging trees and past the flower-gardened houses of the descendants of the English and Irish who migrated from Barbados years ago. On the top, at Sugar Hill, you'll have a wonderful view down over the harbour as well as across on the Atlantic side to the islands of Mustique, Balliceaux, and Battowia (south to north).

Here the road splits in two. Take the high road to the left for a spectacular vista of the islands of the Grenadines which recede to the south, each one fainter as if in deference to the one before – first Isle à Quatre, then Canouan, then sharp-peaked Union, and, on a clear day, in the far distance, recumbant Carriacou.

When the road curves right look down on your left to U-shaped Hope Bay. If you are not tempted to check out this windward beach, take the road which cuts off here to your right, the Lower Mount Pleasant road, which will carry you across pastureland past the Old Fort Hotel to Sugar Hill and down the way you came.

For **Hope Beach**, continue to the end of the paved road at Captain King's house. Turn left on the grass road, pass around the gate intended to keep cattle from straying, and on down the swath of grass which once was a road, past the last house on your right, zig-zagging with the road which erosion has

Coming up from Princess Margaret Beach (OPPOSITE)

The islands of the southern Grenadines from Mount Pleasant. In the foreground are Petit Nevis and Isle à Quatre; in the distance from left to right: Canouan, Carriacou, Mayreau and Union (BELOW)

transmuted into a scree of stones. For future reference in case you come back this way, take your bearings where the trees end and a grassy field begins.

On the beach you'll find seafans and debris washed up by the Atlantic. The expanse of sand is lovely and, if you are in the company of strong swimmers, tumbling in the surf is great fun. If you wish to go back a different way find the trail behind the abandoned beach house at the extreme north end of the beach, which joins up almost immediately with the rough Hope Road, for a hot plod up to Camel and then the pleasant descent into Port Elizabeth.

3   L'An Chemise (L'Anse de Chemin)

One hour each way from Park Bay, but only for the hardy hiker – really away from it all. Take a thirst quencher, and your mask and snorkel if you can manage it. If you are hesitant about finding your own way ask Ricky Nichols at Industry to be your guide.

Follow the road along Park Beach but, before reaching the house perched on the north-east point, take the road left through the coconut grove in a northerly direction up the hill. A turn-off leads to a quarry but you continue on until you reach a very rough road at right angles leading off to the right. Proceed up this a scant 100 yards when you will see on your left a path leading into the woods gently up the slope of the hill. Inhale the perfume (pinch the leaves) of the bay tree, called 'Cinnamon' by Bequians, which dominates the vegetation. Beware, however of the dread brazil bush of the prickly holly-like leaves (see illustration above). Just a graze will give you an unforgettable blistering.

As you come into the clearing at the top of the hill note where you came from for reference on your return as several paths converge here. Proceed over and down the trail on the opposite side towards the sea which you will

The dreaded brazil, do not touch!

glimpse through a lattice of aerial roots dangling from the tall trees. Soon you emerge into an expanse of bright green guinea grass sloping down to the pebble beach at L'An Chemise.

Beautiful varicoloured rocks line the shore; in the distance you see St Vincent across the channel. Surprisingly this now deserted anchorage was once the shipping port of Bequia sending off the agricultural products of the island, such as sugar, indigo and cotton during the time of French domination, (1719–1763) – hence the name L'Anse de Chemin, Bay of the Road, which has since evolved into L'An Chemise. There is very good snorkelling, and the swim will refresh you for the walk back to Park and your waiting transportation, or a further hour's walk back to the harbour.

4 The Roundabout Road to Spring

Two hours for the circuit. If you prefer sticking to the road, but like a good long walk, this is the hike for you.

Take the Spring Road leading out of Port Elizabeth that passes behind the High School but, immediately before you reach the point where it divides in two (the left down to Spring, the right to Hope), take the road to Cinnamon Garden that cuts off sharply to the left up the hill. Notice on your right a fine view over Spring Valley and the far lapping surf of the bay, silent at this distance.

You pass two roads leading off left, one to the suburb of Level, and the other to the Tannis house on top of the hill. Stay with the road which veers right, through stands of white cedar trees and bay trees until you can see down into Spring Valley again. Here take a short detour up a steep spur of the road which gives you a spectacular view of the mainland of St Vincent across the channel. Then continue down the hill almost to the bottom where you take the road left that leads you down again coming out at the northern end of Spring Beach.

If you turn left here you are heading to Industry Bay, but turn right and feel small as you plod along under very tall coconut trees most certainly older than you, that border the length of the beach, past Spring Hotel, and on into Port Elizabeth.

So there you are – some of the many ways to get your exercise in Bequia. That is if you can stir yourself beyond the two-minute cool-off dip in the sea followed by a reapplication of sunblock, which seems to be the maximum level of activity that is enjoyed by you sun worshipers.

Not that you should feel guilty, of course. In Bequia 'liming' or doing nothing is the most popular sport of all!

Five men in a boat, plus ghetto blaster

The music scene

If there is music and people dance you can call it a 'jump-up' or, simply, 'the action'. This, Bequia's favourite form of entertainment, usually involves an electrically-amplified band, either one of the Bequia bands, 'New Direction' or 'Forward', or a St Vincent band such as 'Exodus' or 'Black Sand'. If you attend one of these energetic sessions at a hotel or restaurant, or at the High School, forget conversation – the decibel level will discourage any major foray in that direction anyway – and just enjoy this display of enthusiastic sensuality locked into hypnotic rhythms.

Dancing, that primeval celebration of the human body, seems to come from somewhere more profound even than sex. In Bequia the rhythm of reggae or soca has only to touch the ears of a child of two or three for he or she to break out immediately into a sur-

prisingly expert hip-grinding motion. Old men and women make a good show of it too, much to everyone's delight. One of the highlights of recent entertainment was the 'Old Queen' show at the high school in which attractive ladies of a certain age wowed the audience with their impressive talents.

Bequians love to dance and they do it superbly – with grace, subtlety and a sense of humour. Their relaxed but controlled style is the envy of many a visitor. No flailing about, or jumping up and down for them. It's the least effort with the most punch.

If you are tempted to learn this local body language remember a couple of things. The centre of your body, the fulcrum, is somewhere above your waist and below your sternum. (Isn't that where the soul is supposed to be?) Keep that pivotal spot absolutely

The 'Old Queen' contest sponsored by the Bequia Anglican High School to raise funds was a big success. Here Mrs Rosetta John shows her casual wear outfit

steady, as if your life depended on it, and move everything else around it. And – just as compulsory – keep your whole foot on the floor. No flitting about on tippy toes. So – steady the fulcrum, shuffle the feet, and move it, baby, move it!

Old folks in Bequia remember moonlight fêtes on the pasture above Port Elizabeth that would last all night. In those days, before electricity, 'dark night' saw everyone locked indoors by 8.00 pm (safe from the 'jumbies') so that moonlight was a special time. Music was made on home-made goatskin banjos, and with bamboo flutes of all sizes, and four-string quattros from South America. Later the odd violin, saxophone and big drum would be added to expand the sound. Dances tended to be quadrilles, waltzes, polkas, and the four-step 'shottee'.

A kind of calypso existed amongst the ordinary people which they called 'bungay'. Rather than 'cuss' someone openly they would put their feelings into song. The lady who won her man from her best friend would taunt her whenever she dared to come around:

T, t, turn back, Ophelia,
I'm a b, better woman than you.

These songs could be mischievously insulting:

Me na name Miss Too Wayward,
Gal yo bubby like mash-ee-down,
Then yo foot like a ocean plough,
Look yo head like a dry weather grass,
Me na name Miss Too Wayward.

A rough translation of this could be, 'I won't say who that loose woman is, but her breasts hang down as if someone walked on them, and her feet are splayed like a sea anchor, and her dried up hair has no life in it.' Nothing subtle about those similes!

Calypso began in St Vincent, no doubt under the influence of a similar development in Trinidad, in the early part of this century. Musicians would entertain their governors and social superiors with flattering songs often spiced with satire and humour. It was easier to make critical remarks in music than in the spoken word. This tradition may be heard today in such political calypsos as Trinidad's *Captain the ship is sinking*, and St Vincent's *Horne fuh dem*.

Soca, which developed out of calypso, has a faster dance beat with less emphasis on the words or the message. These are party songs, often good-naturedly obscene, with plays on words or their rhymes, and *double*

entendres, or both, as in *Move your front*, by the band Touch, which purports to be about driving your car. Road marches for St Vincent's annual festival, *Carnival*, are usually a soca tune such as the favourite of 1992, *Pussman*, also by Touch, and Beckett's internationally popular, *Teaser*.

The Rotary Club of Bequia encourages local songwriters and musicians by sponsoring a calypso king contest for the Bequia carnival. Some notable Bequia songs are *Athneal is the greatest whalerman* by Eldon Hazell, *Don't take it out* (on your woman) by Jerome Tannis and *Coal pit* by Clyde Simmons.

Bequia Carnival falls around the end of June, two weeks before St Vincent Carnival – which was moved a few years ago from its traditional time at the beginning of Lent to July in order not to compete with Trinidad Carnival. Songs from all these carnivals are eagerly taken up by the Bequia bands, a yearly addition to their repertoires.

The reggae music you hear originated in Jamaica out of African and West Indian roots and was made popular by the great Bob Marley. Its slower tempo gives heavy stress to the third of the four beats in the bar. The subject is often serious, addressing universal issues as in *No woman no cry* and *Songs of freedom*.

Then there is 'dub' music, much favoured by Rasta musicians. Words are all important – they outline problems of everyday life sometimes with a dose of humour, but generally in a harsh manner. The melody is a repetitive chant. A 'dub' tape will carry on its reverse a 'version' which is without words so you can put your own ideas to the music.

Country music was surprisingly popular in Bequia long before it became so worldwide. Most fans listen on cassettes but the string band, 'De Real Ting', can belt out a mean country tune when they are in the mood.

Bequia's Calypso King, Bernard Hazell, best known as J Gool, singing the favourite We Are Number One

This string band music with unamplified guitar, banjo, quattro, mandolin and tambourine, is the successor, surely, to the entertainment at those moonlight fêtes of yore. Now supported by the hotels and restaurants which regularly employ them, these musicians retain the old skills while featuring many new types of music from pop, to reggae, to soca.

It was Trinidadians who first adapted old oil drums to invent steel band music. The bass player, for example, thumps with two sponge-ball-tipped sticks on six different drums ranged around him, each producing a different note according to the size of the bump hammered onto its top. The 'tune pan', on the other hand, which carries the melody is a single pan cut off to about six inches in

Avondale Leslie leads the string band, De Real Ting, as it stirs up a motley crowd at Gingerbread (ABOVE)

The tune pan, Rising Star Steel Orchestra (LEFT)

depth with more than a dozen bumps, or notes, hammered onto it. With many different-sized pans between these two, an ingenious pan orchestra is formed. Part of its distinctive sound is the result of the fact that when a note is knocked the sound does not continue or sustain itself. Therefore to produce a held sound it is necessary to continue beating the note in rapid succession as long as you wish it to be heard. Steelbands in St Vincent (on the mainland) may have as many

recorded four of his original compositions. The cassette is available from the band which plays weekly at Mustique as well as in Bequia. He puts himself in the reggae, soul, disco tradition with a heavy emphasis on lyrics.

Papa Winnie is Bequia's foremost musical success story. Winston Peters (Simmons) began to play pan with the local steel band, at the age of eleven or twelve, in Lower Bay where he was born. In 1974 he went to sea as galley boy on a local schooner, soon transferring to a Greek cargo ship which took him to South America, Africa and Europe. After two years, when he was all of nineteen, he jumped ship in Algeria, and luckily found work on an Italian cruise ship where he would entertain the guests in addition to his regular job. Eventually he stayed ashore in Genoa, hustling to make a living, with almost no knowledge of the Italian language, working around boats in the harbour. In 1977 he went to Milan where he began jamming with friends in the park. No one in Italy had heard the reggae type of music he was playing. He formed a band, The Irie. Singing background vocal was an Italian girl, Liana, who later became his wife. His famous song, *Rootsie and Boopsie*, refers to the nicknames by which his twin daughters are known.

He has just signed a contract with MCA in Germany but continues to live in Milan, with frequent visits with his family to Bequia.

Speaking of the long road he has travelled to get to where he is today Papa Winnie says, 'You really feel the weight when people don't know who you are. In Bequia everyone knows everyone.'

When I happened to be in a disco in Florence a couple of years ago I thought I would try asking the DJ to play Papa Winnie. On it came immediately, *You are my sunshine* . . . sounding just as appropriate on a crowded psychedelic-lit dance floor in Italy, as it does drifting over the sand from De Reef at Lower Bay.

as 50 players, but you will hear smaller versions in Bequia at various restaurants.

The importance of church music and gospel to the Bequia population can be ascertained by listening to the ladies of the church vocalising at full force during service or, even more impressively, a capello, at the graveside during funerals with such beloved old hymns as *Abide with me* and *The day thou givest Lord is over*.

In spite of the apparent natural aptitude of the people, music appears to be a largely underdeveloped resource. Very few Bequians read music or take up an instrument seriously. Singing is the usual means of expression. In the schools the Seven Day Adventists have the most lively music programme.

Colin Peters of the band Forward has

Mangomania

Mango addiction is so common in Bequia that I used to admit that I was a freak – someone who did not care one way or the other about the ubiquitous fruit that yearly becomes an obsession with the majority of the population.

But that was before I lived with a mango tree in my front garden.

There are many varieties in Bequia – the popular Julie (also known as 'grafted', although only one of the types grafted by the Department of Agriculture), the lush Ceylon, the XXL Imperial, the dainty Teacup, the immortal Paul Over, the stringy Horse mango ('Hossy') and countless others only a born Bequian can put a name to.

The tree in my garden is a Cotton mango and, according to the experts who are my daughters, it's the best on the island. They tell me that in a contest once conducted in its very branches my eldest daughter consumed more than sixty. When I confirmed this with her recently she explained, 'But they're small, Mummy.'

It was not their example alone, however, that pushed me over. In June, at the start of the mango season, the daybreak visitations began – small groups of figures in the dawn's early light quietly collecting a portion of the night's booty or, when all the treasure conveniently deployed on the lawn had been claimed, pitching stones to persuade the agreeable fruits to tumble into waiting hands, and mouths.

As you will realise, Bequian mango trees are deemed semi-public property. If it were a crime to steal a mango there would not be a Bequian, I vouch, to plead innocent.

While walking beside a friend who had edged under the Cotton mango one day, I picked up an obviously useless fruit, too hard and green ever to be edible. As I started to throw it aside my friend implored, 'Don't do that, leave it for someone to stone another mango with'. Mangomaniacs evidently look out for one another.

Visitors trying for a mango

I was particularly impressed one moonless night. Glancing out of the window I saw the beam of a torch probing the darkness under the tree. Now who could be so compelled as to search for mangoes at two in the morning? It was only the nightwatchman from a nearby hotel – one of the perks of the job, I expect.

The continuing aura of public esteem surrounding the Cotton mango got to me at last. I stooped one day for a few choice ones presented like a gift on the grass in front of me. I

These children know the best place to eat a mango

did not intend to eat them. I just carried them to the restaurant to make fresh juice. After a while I noticed the staff seemed inordinately pleased on receipt of this daily supply. Soon I was out there early-birding with the rest of my cohorts armed with a plastic bag and my, fortunately good, night vision.

I became sensitive to the announcement of each new bundle of joy. First the rapid slithering swoosh through the leafy birth canal. Then the proud little thump on landing – public at last! Funny I had never noticed this sound before; now I heard it all around Bequia. I even knew the times the trees spoke most – after a shower of rain, first thing in the morning, in answer to a stimulating gust of wind.

And what amazing fecundity! I estimate my tree dropped five or six dozen per day. Over a period of six weeks that is two and a half thousand. Whoosh – thump, whoosh – thump, sometimes several a minute. Whoosh, another windfall – thump, thank you God.

How could I not be seduced by this Bequia manna from heaven? Everyone else had mango on their face all summer. Now me too.

But come next season don't ask where I live. I and a few hundred other aficionados don't really need any help. Of course if pure chance takes you past my tree at break of dawn after a rainstorm some day, well, join the group. We do understand.

Christmas in Bequia

Bequia looks her best at Christmas-time. The bright green vegetation, revitalised by the autumn rain, provides a brilliant background for the flowers of the season – scarlet poinsettia, white flurry of euphorbia, gold Christmas candle. The harbour, raked a brisk blue by the stiff Christmas breeze, is white-dotted with over a hundred yachts. If you check the crackling flags on their sterns you will count over a dozen countries.

Traditionally Christmas in Bequia is not a time for decorating trees or exchanging gifts. Rather it is a celebration, a reason to 'fête', to feast and drink with friends, to have a good time. Every night electric, string or steel bands tempt from the various hotels and

Christmas companions – euphorbia and poinsettia

Bridesmaids ride to the wedding past the Bequia Book Store on Port Elizabeth's main street

Nicholar and Grafton Caine pose for photographs

restaurants. Carollers make the circuit waking up households with the incantation:

Arise and open the door for me
For the coconut tree is a witness for me.

The family, roused, provide encouragement in the form of food and drink or a donation. Even yachtsmen are not immune. Youngsters, some of whom unfortunately could do with a bit of musical instruction, try their luck rowing from boat to boat.

'Nine mornins' is an unusual Bequia custom possibly derived from the trek of the wisemen following the star to Bethlehem. For the nine nights before Christmas, revellers roam the streets and hillsides descending on acquaintances who may be sleeping to urge them to join their carousing.

But the walking and carolling of the old days have given way to bars and discos that stay open all night or reopen at 4.00 am pouring forth reggae and calypso into the night air until first light. Visitors who treasure a quiet night should take care about holidays at this time, or choose somewhere far from the harbour.

The general sleeplessness resulting from these festivities reaches a climax on Christmas Eve. At 11.30 the bells ring for midnight mass at the Anglican and Roman Catholic churches.

Christmas day dawns with blessed tranquility. A Bequian Christmas dinner may be stewed pork, beef, lamb or mutton (goat), green pigeon peas or peas and rice, a variety of 'ground provisions' such as sweet potato, tannia, dasheen and plantain, accompanied by local drinks such as ginger beer, sorrel, or black wine – a home-made fermentation of mixed fruits and burnt sugar. Restaurants, however, offer international fare with roast turkey, steak, fish and lobster.

The holiday season includes one more fling on New Year's Eve or, as Bequians call it, Old Year's Night, before the island returns to its somewhat more sedate norm.

Easter Regatta

The Easter Regatta, organised since 1981 by the Bequia Sailing Club, is a spectacle unique to Bequia. Yachts representing nations from around the world join with the traditional local fishing boats in a four-day celebration of sail.

Yachts competing in the lusty waters around the island range from vintage schooners and island sloops, to custom-designed racing vessels and Grenadines-based charter boats. The simple Bequia handicap system for classifying boats allows any and everyone to compete.

But perhaps the highlight of the weekend is the series of local fishing-boat races. A favourite scene is the start – Le Mans style – from the beach. The crews stand in the shallows holding their boats awaiting the gun – then it's a frenzy as they shove off, tumble in, set the rudder, trim the sails and, to the uproar of the crowd, manoeuvre out among the closely anchored yachts.

Bequia's graceful seine boats are joined in the hard-fought competition by counterparts from the sister islands of Carriacou and Tobago.

Easter Sunday is a day off for the weary yacht crews, and relaxation comes easily on the golden stretch of Lower Bay Beach with the convenient proximity of De Reef, Keegans, Theresa's and other bars. The single-handed around-Bequia race is reserved for this day, and the fishing-boats races, begun at 9.00 am in Hamilton, finish here too, often

with a rollicking dispute over a tack or a tricky manoeuvre.

Then there are the gumboat races. Neat model yachts are carved by Bequia boys from the soft local gumwood and expertly rigged with cotton sails and thread. For a moment you feel distance is deceiving you, so like real yachts they appear as they bob and cut the seas, their taut sails reacting to the slightest change in wind; then you observe the builder/ owner/captain swimming along behind like a helpful, encouraging giant of the sea.

In a class of their own are the coconut boats fashioned from nothing more than the husk of a coconut with a chunk of old iron for

Beaching the boats after a Bequia Sailing Club race

Before the race on Hamilton Beach, Bequia Regatta, 1993 (FOLLOWING PAGES)

We're ready!

a keel and a bright patch of cloth for canvas – stunningly decorative, and incredibly sea-worthy.

Bequia really rocks regatta weekend. With yacht delegations from Barbados and Trinidad and the further Caribbean, with dinghy sailing crews from Carriacou and Tobago, all with accompanying family and friends, plus some hundreds of Vincentians lured across the channel by the promise of action in Bequia, you can expect the whole island to be out to catch the fun. And fête they do, with the grand finale after the prize-giving at the Plantation House.

An almond leaf makes a great little sailboat

Once isolated, Bequia is relishing, now, a sense of community with the rest of the world. Cars, aeroplanes, CDs, videos, electric music and countless other distractions compete to capture the collective imagination.

But on this island, still, nothing does it like sail. To direct a vessel, be she humble or grand, to answer with honour to the wind and the water, remains every Bequia boy's dream, and many a grown man's preferred pastime. In the language of Bequia, 'It's a love!'

Launching of Jack Sprat, *Friendship Bay, 17 October 1993*

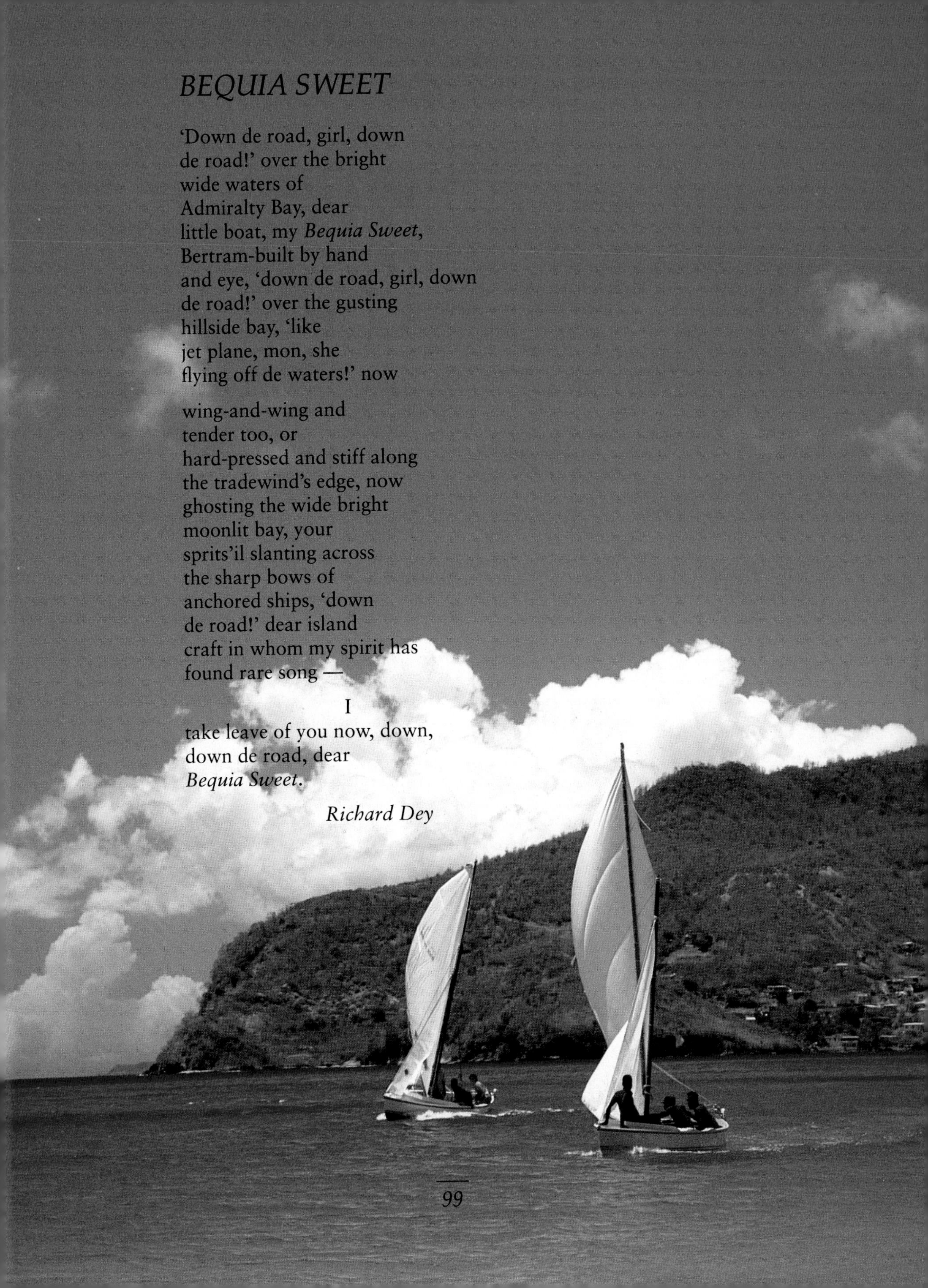

BEQUIA SWEET

'Down de road, girl, down
de road!' over the bright
wide waters of
Admiralty Bay, dear
little boat, my *Bequia Sweet*,
Bertram-built by hand
and eye, 'down de road, girl, down
de road!' over the gusting
hillside bay, 'like
jet plane, mon, she
flying off de waters!' now

wing-and-wing and
tender too, or
hard-pressed and stiff along
the tradewind's edge, now
ghosting the wide bright
moonlit bay, your
sprits'il slanting across
the sharp bows of
anchored ships, 'down
de road!' dear island
craft in whom my spirit has
found rare song —

I

take leave of you now, down,
down de road, dear
Bequia Sweet.

Richard Dey

Recommended reading

I Bannochie & M Light: *Gardening in the Caribbean*, Macmillan Caribbean (Basingstoke), 1993

Virginia Barlow: *The Nature of the Islands*, Chris Doyle Publishing, (USA), 1993

Horace Beck: *Folklore of the Sea*, Wesleyan University Press, (USA), 1973

S Cliff, S Slesin et al: *Caribbean Style*, Clarkson N Potter Publishers, (USA), 1985

Richard Morris Dey: *The Bequia Poems*, Macmillan Caribbean, (Basingstoke), 1988

Chris Doyle: *Sailors Guide to the Windward Islands*, Chris Doyle Publishing, (USA), 1992

Peter Evans: *Birds of the Eastern Caribbean*, Macmillan Caribbean (Basingstoke), 1990

J F Mitchell: *Caribbean Crusade*, Concepts Publishing, (USA), 1989

Neil Price: *Behind the Planters Back: Lower class responses to marginality in Bequia island, St Vincent*, Macmillan Caribbean (Basingstoke), 1988

Douglas C Pyle: *Clean Sweet Wind*, Easy Reach Press, (USA), 1981

Henry Shukman: *Travels with my Trombone: A Caribbean Journey*, Harper Collins (London), 1992

Lesley Sutty: *Fauna of the Caribbean*, Macmillan Caribbean (Basingstoke), 1993

Lesley Sutty: *St Vincent and the Grenadines*, Macmillan Caribbean (Basingstoke), 1993

Lesley Sutty: *Seashells of the Caribbean*, Macmillan Caribbean (Basingstoke), 1990